Ghost of A Dog

Steven Anthony George

Published by Steven Anthony George, 2022.

This is a work of fiction. Similarities to real people, places, or events are entirely coincidental.

GHOST OF A DOG

First edition. October 10, 2022.

Copyright © 2022 Steven Anthony George.

ISBN: 979-8215673973

Written by Steven Anthony George.

Table of Contents

I. A Girl and Her Dog 1
II. From Delphi 9
III. The Food of The Dead 21
IV. Fresh Flower Vending Machine 33
V. Those We Say We Love 45
VI. Reverie 59
VII. Gradus ad Parnassum 67
VIII. Pandora 85
IX. How Terrible Is Wisdom 95
X. "Who's he when he's at home?" 103
XI. The Wine-Pourer 109
XII. Anubis 125
XIII. The Devouring Place 137
XIV: Lullabye 143
XV. Dagger of The Mind 145
XVI. Carmen et Error 151

For Travis

~

Steven Anthony George

~

O Rose thou art sick.
The invisible worm,
That flies in the night
In the howling storm:
Has found out thy bed
Of crimson joy:
And his dark secret love
Does thy life destroy.
  -William Blake

~

~

I. A Girl and Her Dog

"Winter will be here soon, so ensure your best friend has a warm, dry place to sleep, off the floor, away from all drafts, and most importantly, *in your home!* A cozy pet bed with a warm blanket or pillow is ideal. Remember, if it's too cold for you, it's probably too cold for your pet, who can suffer frostbite and hypothermia, just like *you*. So, keep your pets *inside*.

"A message from the Ad Council."

It's like that. It took me a few seconds to find the right button—in the corner, top, right—but I did turn the TV off. I had to think for a minute, try to roll the thoughts around.

Is dying a quick death better than living with unending pain? I think most would say "yes, of course it is." That's an easy decision to make. That's what we all want if we can get it—a quick and easy death.

If there must be pain, then it should be for only a second or two before peace. That's the choice in every book that offers it: Kill me! Have mercy! It should be an even easier choice when it's not your own pain or your own death—not directly—but it's *not easier*. It wasn't easier at all.

The scent of impending rain had hung in the air for a while, however long that was. I recognize that smell. That's how I know most things for certain. The scents, the sights, and sounds, no matter how faint, and that's been giving me a sense of peace. I'd have felt more at ease if it weren't for the red and blue lights alternating on and off outside the window. They'd been there since last night or so, flashing but muted through the curtains, pulsing like a heartbeat—red, blue, red, blue, red, blue—through both the curtain and the blinds like an amusement park funhouse. I first thought it was possible that the lights were from a communication tower of some kind on one of the mountains in the distance, with an aircraft warning light on top, but they moved closer, and then farther away and from place to place.

I'd lived in this house for many years when I was younger and visited many times after that. Still, there were no flashing lights until a night or two ago, at least I hadn't noticed them, but that's expected under the circumstances. Everything I remembered, I remembered out of order and it was a jumble at times.

When I first began to lose myself to the thing, I tried to write, in a form of a story, the few memories that stuck with me like a sliver under my fingernail. I could then read it back later, but to whom? To anyone who would listen I suppose. I'd be proud to do it even for myself because I could read my own words, if they were mine, and I was truly seeing these memories in my own mind's eye.

I've never seen a lighthouse with my own eyes, but I've never been to the ocean either, even though it was no more than a three-hour drive away. I'm not sure why Mom and Dad never went there when I was a boy, but we didn't take many trips in the car, not after they were married. Most kids I knew growing up went to theme parks or took plane trips across the country to a grandparent's house, but my parents stayed in town most of the time, unless Mom took me with her to her doctor's appointment. Neither were close to their own parents or siblings, if Dad had any, and rarely talked about them. We didn't go on outings to the beach, or to cabins in the mountains together, and when I was out on my own, there weren't many opportunities.

Abby was in the next room, and I wasn't sure yet about what to do with her. I left her sitting in the kitchen with a coloring book and crayons, while I was thinking it over, but I had locked the door with all three latches, just so she wouldn't wander off. She didn't seem to want to leave then, so maybe she'd become accustomed to me finally. I spent the first day she was at the house hunting through the bottom of the closet to find toys to keep her entertained.

When she was very little and we were still in the apartment, I would take her to the lake and push her around the park until she got tired, and then we'd go back home and fall asleep for a couple of hours. If the weather was bad, or after it was dark, I'd put a movie on and, even though she wasn't yet two and too young to understand. She'd watch it, fascinated, until she fell asleep, but by September this year, I wasn't driving anymore and electronics were getting complicated for me. I couldn't remember which buttons were for which functions, but I liked the feel of the remote in my hand, and music and TV shows were a nice distraction. That was all I could say for certain.

At the bottom of a basket of clothes in the hall closet, I found the knitted rag doll with the ear-to-ear grin that Dad bought for Abby when she was born. I thought it was a strange thing to buy for a newborn, but I put it in the crib with her when she went to sleep, and she got used to having it. It became one of her favorite toys to carry around when she first started to stand and walk. She'd laugh every time my dad touched her nose with it when we came to visit. It had a smell like raw liver when I found it, and it was stained here and there. The tips of its hands and feet were almost black from play. It had a hat at one time, but that went missing somewhere. With a little difficulty, I put it through the washer with some towels to freshen it, but the machine tore it to pieces. I became dizzy and thought I would throw up when I picked the stuffing out, though I'm not sure I could say why.

There were a few other small toys in the closet, but they were all baby things. She was too old for any of them, but they were all I could find in my current condition. I had given her peanut butter on toast for dinner, because it wasn't too difficult to fit bread into the slots of the toaster and I wasn't sure I could handle anything more complex. After I made sure she could keep herself busy at the kitchen table, where she seemed content for now, I went back to the living room and sat down on the couch.

Bernadette was going to be in the hospital again for at least a few days. I missed her, but I was here with Abby, just my little girl and me, alone together in my own house, the house Dad left to me. Bernadette and I finalized the divorce a month or so before he had the accident, so it was good that he left it for me, because I feared the other options. Now having Abby here too gave me the opportunity to end all of this for everyone, and anyone that was unfortunate enough to earn my love. I probably wasn't capable of love now in any normal sense, but I felt that I still needed someone. There was an emptiness, even after all this. So maybe if I did what it urged me to do, I would also be free.

I couldn't prove the judge wrong when Bernadette decided to spend time apart barely a year after we were married. She wanted a court separation, saying that she'd feel "safer with that."

"I'm going to take Abby and stay with my mother and Dad for a while."

"It's not fair. It was a mistake."

"You don't put sharp... Never mind. It's just a while."

I don't know. I can't remember most of the details. Whatever the details were, they weren't created by God.

She wanted six months to think about what to do next.

"Come on, Vinny, it's six months! We'll be around to see you."

So, she took Abby, who just started crawling then, and stayed with her parents. I stayed at the apartment. She brought over money to help each month. It almost killed me to have them away, but it was only for a half a year. When did she come back, Abby was walking already and creeping up and down stairs, but Bernadette wasn't the same fun or funny girl she was and that was even before the visit to Dad's—well, here now—a few days later.

The judge was a woman, of course, and didn't want me to keep Abby half the time as I was asking for. "Mr. Pelletier, I find little evidence that you are responsible enough to care for yourself, much less an infant without help," she said.

Okay, I do make mistakes, but why? What was it about me that made most women treat me like trash? Bernadette's mother, Gabriella, was sweet to me, or at least until she felt that she had good reason to be otherwise. Until then, I counted on her as someone I could call to talk. One other didn't treat me badly either, really. I'm not sure why she's come to mind just now.

That I was irresponsible was the judge's conclusion based on Bernadette's report without even talking to me, but I was myself then, of course, and I was doing all right. I had my own thoughts and ironed my clothes for court. I gained some muscle because I was working out at a gym before work four days a week and I looked good. My hair was a little long, but the girls liked when it was shaggy, and I took care of it.

Judge Gorniak would have liked me even less if she knew I no longer had a job, but I was the one option left for Abby, with Bernadette in the hospital and her parents in poor health. I can't imagine how the judge would feel about me if she'd been the fly on those sunshiny walls when I visited the priest last August. That was too late to make any difference, but if it had gone as I hoped, it would have confirmed what I thought. Maybe what he said was right, but I wasn't sure yet about what.

It was mid-November, so it had gotten dark early, and I thought it was later than it was. I did find one of my coloring books and a box of crayons from when I was little in the bottom kitchen drawer, and I gave those to Abby. While she colored in the kitchen, I watched spots of colored light that were projected onto the living room wall by the stained-glass lampshade that Gabriella gave us when we moved into the apartment. Bernadette didn't think it fit with the décor there, so it stayed in the closet, and I took it with my things when I moved out. The lights quivered ever so slightly as if there were a minor earthquake, though there was none that night and there hadn't been one for many years. A pack of coyotes howled together in the distant brush. It was shrill and piercing like the voice of the thing, though less terrifying, but given how close I was to satisfying its demands, I hadn't heard it all day.

I stood up. I kicked away a few plastic grocery bags on the floor and went out to the kitchen where I left her. I sniffed her hair and it smelled musky. She must have used that fox pelt from what was my dad's office as a pillow again when she took her nap. She turned and smiled. I kissed the top of her head. A raccoon, I suppose, knocked over a trashcan somewhere outside and it startled me. I took a few deep breaths. I felt nauseated and weak, as if I had just woken up from a long nap.

"Want to be brave with me, Abby? Let's go down and we can be brave together."

She continued to color.

"All right?" I asked.

She held the crayon still and looked at me from the corner of her eye, then she nodded, at first with hesitation, and then more eagerly, until she almost smiled and took my hand. I was relieved. She looked better than she did in the morning when she was crying because the pain in her side came back worse than the day before. She called it the "chewing pain" and she was asking for her mommy again.

I was expecting something like that eventually, but the pains didn't start until yesterday after the social worker dropped her off. Knowing she was coming, I smoothed my hair down and tried to look as much like myself as possible, but I knew I didn't smell good because I caught my own stink without ever losing it. I sprayed myself with cologne, which was so intense to me that I gagged, but the woman never came to the door, so I had to go out to look for her. Maybe she had missed the house. So many look alike on the street and some don't have numbers that are plain to see.

The social worker—names, I couldn't remember them unless I heard them over and over—never spoke to me, or I didn't see her, or I just don't remember that she was here. She'd wandered off somewhere—it looked that way—leaving Abby at the front of the house when I brought her in. She didn't meet with me at all. Is that normal? Did it happen that way? Am I any judge of what is meant to be normal on any day anymore? If anything worked as it normally should I wouldn't be thinking what I was thinking, or what we are or were thinking. Consecutive and logical strings of thoughts meant nothing. So, there was that.

Maybe I did forget. I've done a lot of that, but I hoped that that time and that night, I could follow through with what I knew was the only thing I could do and finish it in a flashing second, before I could change my mind. No. Wait. It's not my mind, not so much.

Abby jumped down from the chair and rubbed her nose. We crossed the kitchen, hand-in-hand to the basement doorway. I had left the door open all that afternoon purposely. It was less of a threat. I felt okay doing that. It was, from all I learned, all I had left to do and the only choice anyone had left me with.

If I'd ever learned how to load the rifle properly, or if I even had the guts to fire it, that might have been quicker and more certain, but I wouldn't keep Dad's gun where anyone, including me, could reach it easily, because I was afraid I would use it on myself, and I knew I couldn't do that, but even locked in a chest in the attic, the temptation would be too great. Going off into the woods and blowing the top off my head seemed the easiest and fastest solution. I'd make sure it was somewhere secluded, maybe a mile in, where they wouldn't find my body until the animals and elements had their way with my bones, but I had to think of the others and that endless physical pain I would have left them to live through. So, this was the only answer—the only solution the thing offered me. I'm so sorry. I'm sorry, in my heart, for all of this, but it would never allow me to do anything else.

If I pushed Abby hard, without warning and with enough force, she might never realize what happened. Maybe she would think she tripped, because to believe, even for a second, that the man you called "Daddy"—though she never yet called me that—was killing you, would have to be more horrible than the dying, but maybe at her age she had no sense of what death was yet, like I didn't have a sense of what life was anymore.

II. From Delphi

The interchange was seamless
   imperceptible to most.

I poked my finger between those lines in the poetry book sometime in September, which was about four months after the thing entered me and about three months after my Dad died; maybe it was later. I couldn't read more than a few words by that point—around the time of Gabriella's birthday. I bought her a card with a child-like drawing of sunflowers printed on it, but it never left the house. Maybe later. Weird. Confusing. It was the first time that the oracle made little sense to me, but that was where I was.

I was walking everywhere by then, but wherever I needed to go seemed far away, so that I wanted to run instead, though my legs weren't working as they once did. Sometimes, I wanted to rush out the door, but to where? I didn't know, but I wanted to just keep running. Wherever I went, the thing was with me, because I was not in charge of myself, if I even knew who I was. But it led me to this book, I think. Was it my own finger pointing the way, or was it the thing that guided my finger to the spot? Either way, the direction was correct, because everything would be all right. That was what I remembered.

Did you learn nothing? You will be sorry!

Maybe the lines were veiled to me because I chose a poetry book, and so it was already abstract or metaphorical, something inscrutable, but I had used many types of books, even a magazine, and a bit of junk mail once before. Every time, the results worked perfectly with no uncertainty, even if they offered only a new perspective that I could apply to the situation I was in, but I was asking for a specific solution. I couldn't wrap my mind around a line so complex by then, but it would come to me.

The minute I got home from Gabriella's house after that visit to her, I stabbed my finger at the newspaper spread open on the coffee table and looked down to see that I had landed on the Dear Abby column by Abigail Van Buren. To be honest, even at that point, even after we were married, I wasn't certain Bernadette would keep the baby, but the name was so clear and plain, I was sure that she would. That afternoon, we picked up the keys to our apartment, and I asked her then how she felt about the name "Abigail" if the baby were a girl. I was sure that it would be, otherwise the paper would have led me to another name. She said that she loved that name and always had. It had chosen right.

When Bernadette first got pregnant, she'd pace the carpet with her hand in her hair.

"My mother'll kill me right on the spot when she finds out," she said.

But over time, as each week passed, Bernadette warmed more to the idea of being a mother, and then the natural maternal instincts took over. I saw that glow that I'd heard of. Bernadette's cheeks were rosier by the day, and she smiled more often. By the time she started to wear maternity clothes, she was excited about buying tiny one-piece outfits, a crib, bottles, diapers, a changing table, and a mobile of various circus animals—a lion, a pony, a monkey, and a bear under an umbrella top. I decorated the room on the same theme, by covering the walls with adhesive animal appliqués, though I couldn't get half of them to stick.

Getting married was something we did more for the sake of the baby than ourselves, but I would have proposed to her eventually even if she hadn't been pregnant, because I was in love with her. My dad wanted to be a granddad at some point, but I loved Bernadette's mother, Gabriella, like she was my own, and would never disappoint her. I didn't want to disappoint anyone if I could help it. I wanted to be a man and take responsibility for the girl I gave my heart to. Bernadette was the only girl I spent any real time with in the real world.

The only other girl I felt love for, was a Colombian student from the college, but it was only once that we got to be together. I stopped by her apartment a few times after the night I spent with her and no one would answer the door until the last time, when a fat, sweaty bald man came to the door and told me to go away. So, she must have moved away somewhere, maybe back to Colombia, but I think of her sometimes.

This was the first time, in the previous five or so years I was using the book this way that I needed to roll a sentence over in my mind many times, taking it apart, word for word. It had to be something symbolic, a puzzle to solve, or a clue to the puzzle itself. I decided to dissect it, beginning with the opening phrase. "*The interchange*" made some sense; things had changed, but *"was seamless"* implied a substitution, one that I may need to make, and was *"imperceptible,"* maybe even to me, but what was and was not real was already becoming blurred, like my vision was over time, but only at times. That much gave me some satisfaction, but I needed to try to focus on what it meant, and eventually I would understand. It seemed I needed a substitute in some way.

I would understand this puzzle in the end, as it happened with that tarot card reader at the county fair, about two months after mom died, and I wasn't yet fourteen. The card reader told me what I'd already known. All the theatrics that came with it weren't necessary because I was ready and willing to listen, but she also told me what I *didn't* know. Eventually, I would understand all those things.

The tarot card reader had set up shop inside a green and white tent in a choice location near the front of the fairgrounds, between the big, orange beer tent, which was set off a few yards behind it with all the whooping, fat drunks who could get their beer cheaper at any bar in town, and another tent in the same colors, but much larger, displaying the new technologies and best careers of the year. An A-frame chalkboard outside the fortuneteller's tent read, "Tarot readings. Past Lives and Dark Energies. For Entertainment Only."

I walked in with a canvas tote I bought at the fair's entrance that contained toys, mementos, and crafts I paid for at the vendors' booths in the red barn, to find a light hanging on a hook with netting covering it to dim it. The card reader and another person were sitting on two sides of a folding table. The reader looked up, maybe a bit angrily. "Give us a few minutes," she said, then took a breath and smiled. "I am still with a customer."

"I'm sorry. I can wait," I said.

"I will call you in," she said.

"I didn't know."

I gazed across the grounds to the Ferris wheel, the same one as last summer—it looked like the one I remembered—lit with its red and blue lights, and on the other side, the Tilt-a-Whirl, and the Scrambler. Two years earlier, I saw a girl and her mother hurt on the Scrambler when a screw came loose while the car was in motion. They had no serious injuries, but it was reason enough to stay off them. The rides made me sick in any case, so they weren't fun. I didn't like any of them. There was the loud hard rock of the Skee-Sleds from the very back of the grounds, a contraption that spun suspended cars at high speeds in a rising and falling circle. That terrified me the one time that I rode it, and I never did set foot on that ride again, but I liked listening to the music.

The scent of crispy waffles dusted with powdered sugar hung in the air, and then the intense cinnamon candy that pretty girls dipped Granny Smiths in, sausages and peppers from the Knights of Columbus's concession, and birch beer and steak sandwiches from Kiwanis. Everyone was making money from something that smelled like no food anyone ever got at home. If not that confectionary, then they'd make their money from something frightening, loud, or unfair. If not that, then they at least got ribbons in places that smelled like hay and manure. I was prickly under my tee-shirt from the heat and humidity. Maybe I was pricklier that summer because Dad didn't do laundry the way Mom did. None of my clothes felt soft anymore. They smelled more like seaweed than rose petals, so Dad was doing something different.

A recorded, muffled male voice announced over a P.A. system a sideshow act—something distorted—human oddities? —followed by the words "Aliiiive, aliiiive, aliiiive!" repeatedly. I could never understand every word over the speakers, but it was the same each year. I thought freak shows were a thing of the past, when people were either incasts or outcasts and there was no in-between, but people make money however they can with the talents they have to work with, and if they don't mind it, no one else should.

After the length of one of the Skee-Sled heavy metal songs, the card reader's customer, a short, muscular man with thick black hair, and a dark complexion, emerged from her tent, glancing at me for a second, and then looked to the ground, as if he were embarrassed to be seen, and a minute later, the fortuneteller emerged.

"Come, come," she said, gesturing with her hand.

I smiled at her and walked inside again. The card reader smiled as well and asked me to sit down. She wore a red floral dress that exposed a tattoo of a broken heart on her shoulder, and a sheer shawl with feathers sown onto it. She also wore a round hat that looked something like a lampshade with fringe hanging from it, that partially covered her eyes. She appeared younger than I would have thought most fortunetellers would be. Her makeup was garish, for exotic effect I suppose, and so it was hard to tell for sure what her real age was, especially in the lighting.

On the interior tent wall behind the fortuneteller were strings of red Christmas lights and on the grassy floor below them, a large, polished brass vase with giant paper flowers in it.

"What is your name?"

"Vincent, or Vinny. Both are okay with me."

"How old are you?"

"Thirteen. Am I too young to do this?"

"I can't take money from you without an adult with you."

"My dad is out on the grounds somewhere, but he gave me money to do w-what I wanted here today, so I thought—"

"Do you know where he is?"

"—Please—"

"Maybe if he came in too."

"I th-thought I would see what you did. He told me to meet him at the front gate at five o'clock and it's still only about four now."

"Still..." She twisted her mouth up in a strange way.

"I-I did everything else I could do already. I bought a silver ring with a dragon on it, and made my own painting in the pavilion, but I don't like rides, and I'm not good at the games, so I still have most of my money left."

"I'm obligated to tell you that, as far as you're concerned, it will be for fun. You understand?"

"But you have real faith in what the cards tell you, right?"

"Yes, of course, but you need to keep a perspective."

"That doesn't mean I won't learn anything. There are a few things I need to know. Please?"

"I'm afraid you'll take too much to heart with this."

"It's what you do, right? You tell fortunes."

The lady smiled and pulled away from the table a bit. "I don't tell fortunes so much as I tell you what you should expect. Does that make sense?"

"Yes! That's exactly what I thought!"

The card reader went silent, then scratched her shoulder.

"All right, Vinny, it'll be twenty dollars, and we'll see what the cards have to say."

My denim cutoffs were a bit too tight because I was growing out of them, and I was also sore, so I had to stand, but I dug the cash out of my pocket. There were several smaller crumpled bills, and I peeled them apart to find a twenty. I handed the cash to her, and she dropped it into a Japanese-style urn next to her chair.

First, she scattered the cards with her right hand only in a face-down jumble across the table, and then gathered them up into a neat deck again. She next laid the deck of cards on the table and asked me to cut them in what felt like the right place for me.

"How will I know?" I asked.

"It's a matter of trusting your intuition."

I cut the cards at the spot where it seemed correct.

She picked up the deck from the table, and then laid the cards out onto the table in a cross pattern with three or four others to the side of it.

"Hm." She frowned. "I can see that you've suffered a great loss. And you are having a difficult time adjusting to the changes that are taking place because of that loss," she said in a kind voice.

Maybe she was real.

"Yes, that's true!" I said with anticipation.

"But this difficult period will pass, and then you will find that you are more at peace with yourself than you were before."

That was an easy comment for her to make.

"That's all there is?" I asked.

"We have five to ten minutes."

She held up the card that she pointed to and showed it to me.

"Can I look at it?" I asked and tentatively reached out to touch it.

She turned the card toward her face, frowning at it for a moment and then hesitantly offered it to me, face up.

"Are your hands clean?" she asked.

"Yes," I said. "I'm too careful about washing my hands sometimes. I might be obsessive. I don't know."

She looked at me in the eyes and then handed over the card reluctantly, her mouth shut like a clamp.

I held it by the edges and looked down at it.

There was a church of some kind in the background, with a stained-glass window and a carving or statue—an effigy, they're called—of a knight that lay upon a tomb.

"Those swords are a reminder of the suffering that he has endured in the *Three* of Swords," the card reader said. "The struggles have ended, and a new phase begins. That is where you are."

"Are you a psychic?" I asked.

"Can I see your future?"

"Yes, can you tell me what *will* happen?"

A fly buzzed left and then right across my face so close that I could feel the air turbulence. I watched it, but luckily, it didn't land on me.

"I told you, Vinny. Your future is up to you."

"I don't feel like it is. I think I'm cursed."

"Are you afraid of the future? Some are, at your age."

"I'm afraid of my present. I'm not afraid of my future."

"You are still young."

"Yes, I suppose that if I were a very old man, I might be afraid. When you're old you have less future."

"Are you afraid of death?" she asked.

"I'm afraid of what they do with your body after that."

"Death's a part of life. All life ends. We have our time."

"But little children die every day," I said. "Sometimes in pain. That seems unfair."

"Few things in life are fair, Vinny, but we learn lessons from it."

"I'm not sure what the lesson is for the parents."

Again, the tarot card reader looked annoyed. "You will live a long, happy life, I am sure. Do you want to continue?" she asked me.

"Did you read *Slaughterhouse Five*?

"No."

"It's about a time-travelling optometrist."

"That sounds like quite a book for a young man at your age," she said, looking down over the cards. "Do you want to continue? I have to generate business."

"Do you believe in God? I believe in an afterlife, but I'm not sure about God."

"We are here to talk about *you*."

"I think I believe in ancestor worship, like your dead forefathers and foremothers look over you, and so *they* are God."

The card-reader flattened her hand on the table. "Do you have a specific question?"

"Okay. The thing I want to know is why those you love, and those who say they love you, will hurt you to show that they love you."

"That's a deep question, Vinny. Your layout shows me that all will be okay in the end, so maybe what you are going through only requires some patience."

"Mom's not coming back, no matter how long I wait."

The card reader put her hand to her mouth, then laid it back on the table. "Did your mother leave you?"

"Yes!" I said. "She died! On the first day of summer. That's June 21st, right?"

"Oh, I am so sorry to hear that. That was recent. You should have mentioned it."

"But that wouldn't affect what that cards say, right?"

"No, but I might have interpreted their meaning in another direction."

"But Mom's dying's not the problem! Not nearly anymore."

I think we had both forgotten that I still had the card in my hand. I looked back down at it then. Three swords hung on a wall with a fourth sword lying on the tomb of a dead knight. Was he dead? In any case, the scene was peaceful, as if the great fight was over. The knight's hands were positioned as if he were praying. I never prayed. We didn't have that in us.

"It's a pretty card," I said. "I've never seen a deck of tarot cards with my own eyes."

"Some decks are exquisitely painted," the reader said.

"The knight has a tomb outside a church," I said.

"It's *inside* a church."

"No, I don't think so," I said. "We are outside looking in."

"Vinny," she said, taking the card from my hand, "why would the tomb be *outside* the church?"

"What if they didn't want him inside?"

She gave me that same look that women often do, and it made me sorry for asking what I did.

"I guess I used up my time," I said.

"It's only that you don't seem to be focused on the card reading."

"I don't know what to do."

"I see nothing that you should worry about. Your father seems to love you very much, giving you all that money to spend and having the run of the fair. Maybe he's the one who is helping you reach that peace."

The acrid smell of the malt and hops from the beer tent hit my nostrils suddenly, like a wet towel. The direction of the wind must have changed.

"You are an incredibly fragile thing in a reasonably difficult world, and you need to learn to cope with that, because this is the one life you'll have."

She said it the same way that a saleswoman tries to sell you something over the phone.

"I'll get through. I guess I'm done."

"Very well then," she said, gathering up the cards. "You still have forty-five minutes to enjoy yourself. I'm crazy about the banana split funnel cakes, but my waistline is *not*! They're at the last trailer before the midway rides. If I had money to blow, that would be my choice."

I had to wait, but I knew my question about how to cope would be answered in the only way it could be answered—in exactly the way the fortuneteller said it would be, with time and patience, but time would follow me, whether I wanted it to or not. Maybe it was like the other poem with the hunter in the winter in the same book. There were interchanges, and substitutions to make, and time does heal, sometimes not fast enough, but patience has its own schedule. We're responsible for that part, patience, and it's a big responsibility.

III. The Food of The Dead

The thing was a spirit that curled up in the pit of my chest, and committed itself to me, like no one living ever had. It urged me continually to do the one thing I could not do. I refused to do what it wanted, yet the thing insisted every day and night. I began to think maybe there was an answer that was spiritual if there was no other possible way. I thought that if I consulted a priest, someone who would listen and understand, he would hold up a cross and say some phrases in Latin, and its demands would be over, because by the time August came around, I felt that I needed an exorcism of some kind, because I was possessed by this thing. I was possessed enough that I wanted to learn why it had cursed me in the way it did, as much as it must have known how much I wanted to rid myself of it.

Saint Roch Parish Catholic Church was the nearest to me. It would be about fifteen minutes walking, and I wasn't happy that it was even that far. For the fifth day in a row, it was oppressively hot. The temperature had climbed into the upper nineties, and the sky was neon blue and cloudless. It was humid and the sun was blinding. It was a chore to just pull the weeds when they popped up around the hedges. I suppose I shouldn't have cared about yard work anymore, but I did. Pulling the weeds up and trimming the boxwoods was my job when I was a boy, and it became a habit, and so I would pull weeds without thinking about it. I did it like a silent command in my mind, every day, even after I no longer cared about anything else. I wanted to mow the lawn too, almost desperately, but I was afraid of the mower, the motor noise and spinning blades. Still, this kind of thing had to be done. If what is outside is especially pretty, it will hide what's inside.

I'd called St. Roch's hoping the priest there would understand more fully what it was that had taken me. The Catholics have names for various types of demons, each doing some kind of specific harm, and there was a specific saint who had the job of driving away that demon. He'd believe that the thing was in me if no one else did, and that there might be a way to get it out and away, like a kind of magical surgery. I hoped he would understand the supernatural as no one else could.

The priest at the church himself answered the phone when I called, and I was relieved. I couldn't recall his name at the time, because my memory for new information was becoming poor by then, and I could only memorize by repetition, so I repeated it to myself. It will come to me.

I told him all that had happened that night in May on the way home from work, and how it affected me. To my relief, he listened to me and didn't question what I told him. He responded with only "M'hm, m'hm." He then agreed to meet that same day if it were possible. I wrote down the time, "at or near 3:00," and then stuffed the note into my pocket. He asked that I come to the rectory where he lived, which was a yellow brick building next to the church.

A few blocks short of the church was a drug store that I had stopped into three or four times before, a store that sells quaint country décor items— "harvest" plaques —*wash your hands and say your prayers. Jesus and germs are everywhere*—along with the pain relievers and shampoos, and such. I went in for something cold to drink, but as I pulled open the door, I spotted a deer, not so graceful, across the street taking tentative steps to cross.

She seemed confused, though not afraid of the traffic, and even approached the windows of cars as they stopped at the light. I went inside—*autumn skies and apple pies*—where I saw masks and costumes for Halloween already for sale—cowboys and pirates, witches and angels. The walls on that side of the store were paneled in wood. To the back of that aisle was a werewolf mask. I placed the mask over my face, careful not to let it touch my oily, sweaty skin, and then looked at myself in the mirror at the end of the aisle.

I love you, sweet wolf, my wolf. You, cutie.

I returned the werewolf mask to the hook, then grabbed a bottle of water from the cooler near the checkout. I paid and exited back to the street, where the hot air hit me like a wet towel to my face. I drank the water down within a minute or two, the thin plastic bottle collapsing, though I struggled at first to fit the opening of the bottle between my lips. When I got to the churchyard, I pushed my empty water bottle down into the garbage can by the curb. I pressed the button for the doorbell. It didn't buzz or ring, but chimed with three tones, and I smiled. I thought everything would work itself out.

The priest was younger than I imagined from his voice, about my own age, and Filipino, I think. He had dark, wavy hair that was long enough to dust his shoulders. He also had a smooth, hairless face—Father Baylón, maybe that was the name—that made him seem almost feminine. He wore round wire-framed glasses, and he was holding a halved pomegranate that dripped red juice onto the concrete on the stoop when he opened the door.

He invited me in, then led me down a short hall, where he opened an ornate wooden door that opened into a spare room, furnished with two chairs that faced a massive desk and another larger chair. The room smelled of old, yellowed paper. He asked me to sit down at one of the smaller chairs. They were each fitted with a red velvet cushion. I assumed this was the office where he did his daily paperwork, whatever daily tasks priests need to do.

He put the pomegranate half into a white bowl on the blotter, then wiped his hands on a cloth on a hook by the door. The office, although mostly bare, was cheery, and I felt at ease, at first, like I was visiting a friend more than a stranger.

"I like the color," I said, indicating the walls. "It's brighter than I imagined it would be."

"You imagined it would be dark?" he asked, pulling his heavy chair out from under the desk.

"Catholic churches are always dark, at least in movies."

"Sometimes. So, we enjoy a bit of respite from that here. The crew came in to paint it only three months ago. It's called 'Tuscan Sun,'" he said looking it over. "It was a sandy color on the swatch, but it was too yellow for me on the walls." He shrugged. "But it will do."

The priest then leaned forward and pulled in his chair. He smiled at me for a moment, then sat down.

"Now, let me ask you what you know of this spirit you say is inside you," he said, sitting down. "Please feel free to start from the beginning."

"It tells me what I *need* to know," I said. "And nothing else."

"Is it here now?"

"It's here, b-but next to me. It's like that sometimes."

"In the other chair?" he asked, awkwardly pointing to it.

"No. Just around me. It doesn't stay in one place for more than a minute, except when I'm sleeping, then it watches over me."

"M'hm." He smiled at me again and then broke his expression, almost mechanically. "But you can see it?"

"Not so well in the daylight, but I can."

"Ah, okay, yes, and it speaks to you, and you understand it?"

"Not in the way people normally talk."

"Then how *does* it speak to you and what does it tell you?"

"I understand what it means. I know that."

The stained-glass window was at the front of the office facing the sun, and it projected colored light onto the priest's face. It was an image of the Virgin Mary, Jesus' mother. Her arms were open and welcoming. I could never understand the reason for The Church, but I understood the appeal of its figures. It must be comforting to have a mother who's always there to hold us when we need it, one who's eternally present at every moment.

I wasn't ready to tell him that I didn't always understand the thing's language or languages fully, and yet I understood the gist of what it was saying. I was afraid he would blame me, so I remained silent, but he appeared to be impatient with my silence, as if I were refusing to answer.

"What do you do?" he asked, digging seeds out of the pomegranate without spilling them. More red juice flowed around it. The room began to spin a little. I took a deep breath.

"I work nighttime security at a technology warehouse—advanced computer hardware. I-I mean, I did until a few days ago, but I had to take time off because of this. I probably can't go back now."

I felt I was minimizing the problem, so I added, "I don't think that I can, now that I'm not thinking with my own mind."

"M'hm." He shrugged and sat back. "You seem an intelligent man in the way you speak. I thought you might be well-educated."

"I'm always educating myself as much as I can. I used to read a lot."

"Reading is important for everyone. It exercises your imagination. What do you enjoy reading?"

"Nothing lately, of course, but anything but trash novels or anything like that. I tried to read the classics if I could. I enjoyed *Moby Dick*, and *The Catcher in The Rye* very much."

The priest chuckled a bit. "Do you have a favorite?"

"Maybe *The Picture of Dorian Grey*. I forgot that one. I like how it was written."

"That is an impressive list of titles for a man such as yourself, but what did you mean by 'trash novels'?"

"*Popular* novels, I probably should have said, like fantasy stories or science fiction. They don't interest me much."

The priest laughed a bit, but more to himself.

"Many people would not consider fantasy stories trash. I read science fiction."

"*Popular*."

"Nothing wrong with horror and fantasy. It's good to have a bit of fun with the imagination."

"I suppose some are worth the time, but I always liked classics—stuff I can study and learn from, and that takes me to a different time and place."

"We all like to do that at times."

"Earlier this year I was reading a collection by a few local poets that they were selling at the library, and it was soon after that that it happened in the woodlot on the way home from work, like I explained on the phone, and so I haven't read much of anything since then."

"Maybe all the reading is why you have such a way with words," he said, then flashed that brief smile at me yet again.

"But less each day. It's becoming difficult."

I felt uncomfortable as the priest began to scrutinize me.

I continued. "I tried college a few years ago, twice, but I couldn't keep my grades up. I'm better with that imagination part than I am with writing papers or turning them in on time."

"Speaking with you now, you seem on top of things. I am not sure what kind of help you need."

Again, he watched me, not moving nor shifting his gaze.

"It's not anything that anyone can easily see without being in my place."

"And so then, we must get back to this spirit inside you—or around you, correct?"

After collecting pomegranate seeds into his palm, he spilled them into his mouth, and then chewed, crunching them loudly.

"Yes," I began to explain, thinking about each word, an attempt to be clear. "I can smell and hear more acutely. It's even painful at times, but my thoughts, they seem to fade with time, I mean, my thinking. It's taking those."

The priest looked down at the desk for a moment, and then nodded.

"I will ask you, have you seen any animals where you shouldn't see them?" he asked, folding his hands in front of himself on the desk.

"Just on the way here, yes!" I said. "I watched a doe walking along the sidewalk on Market Street before I went into that drug store around the corner to get a bottle of water, but that's not strange. Unusual, I guess."

"Are you sure it was a female?" the priest asked, looking at me from over his small eyeglasses.

"Yes. My father used to go hunting when I was a boy. I know deer and it was a mature doe. There's woodland only about five blocks down from there. Deer sometimes walk into town and even on the street like that, though I've never seen one approach cars."

"Like a whore?" asked the priest as simply and easily as he would ask me which flavor ice cream I wanted. I followed his eyes. He began scrutinizing a bit of plaster coming down off the ceiling over the crucifix on the wall to the right, then I turned back.

It took me a while to put my words together. "W-Why would you say that?"

"The deer, they are whores," he responded, and then waved his hand as if driving off a fly, continuing to focus on the ceiling. He pointed to a spot with two fingers, then corrected himself. "Or the one you're speaking of is."

"You'll have to explain. Maybe it's because I'm not Catholic?"

"You don't need to have a religion at all," he said, "but it's a shame that you have none, because it would be a help to you."

"My wife—ex-wife's family—is Catholic. I don't go to any church, but I believe in a life after death."

He nodded, looking down at his desk, before suddenly looking up again. "Would you care for the other half of the pomegranate? Difficult to eat, but they're good for you." He then looked me in the eye and again the smile, but faintly. "The good things are often difficult."

"No, thank you," I said. "The th-thing about whores—"

"It took a while for me to get used to the hard seeds inside."

"Please, what did you mean?"

The priest shrugged and then frowned.

"There is a prostitute; her name is Maggie. She stayed here at the church during the winter when she was homeless. She has trouble with drug addiction... and with drinking. She's been chased away from the store many times, and when she's not doing well, she approaches the cars asking for money or looking for tricks. That is who you saw. Animals see other animals. It is 'eat or be eaten.' Animals are either prey or are preyed upon."

"I'm not an animal, but as I told you on the phone, I guess I think like one."

When the priest first led me into the office, I hadn't noticed that it wasn't much cooler. Now I realized there was no air conditioning in the room. It was becoming uncomfortably warm, though this didn't seem to bother the priest, even with the collar.

"I'm burning up." I probably muttered that under my breath.

"Are you sure about that?" he asked as I watched him again dig seeds out of the fruit. "What has this thing told you?"

"I don't always get every word." I sensed that the priest was becoming frustrated with me. "Because it has no one language. I-I'm having trouble understanding words myself at times."

"It doesn't want to kill you. Is that correct?"

"Yes, it loves me. It wants me to be alive."

"It needs you to stay alive so that it can feed on those you love – those you say you love."

I tugged at my tee-shirt, around my neckline, because it was becoming sticky. "It loves me, but it hates those I love, in a burning way. It wants me to itself."

"So, it is a jealous spirit," the priest said, sitting forward.

"Yes, a deep, burning, hateful jealousy."

"You said it prefers to torture those you love. 'It wants to gnaw on their flesh slowly and every day.' I believe that is how you described it when you called."

"Yes, it is something like that!" I felt he was beginning to understand. "It is a kind of parasite."

The priest smiled faintly, a bit mockingly, self-satisfied. "You need a psychiatrist, not a priest."

That same warmth I had felt in my chest since the thing entered me three months ago, turned into a hot stone. My mouth went dry.

"So, you think I'm crazy then."

"No, but I can't help you. The position of The Church is that spirits of animals do not walk the Earth. If you were possessed by a demon, then we have an argument for an exorcism... but you must already be aware of the complications, even in that case."

The priest tossed the pomegranate, spent of its seeds, into a wastebasket in the corner, dripping more red juice during its trip. I again went silent, and so did he. The priest watched me with furrowed brows, almost examining me; maybe he felt pity for me. The time that passed then felt like hours, because I wasn't sure of the passage of time anymore. How long had I been there?

Maybe domestic animals have no sense of time, maybe because they were bred for tens of thousands of years to be stupid companions, or sources of work, or food. They know nothing else but that. Maybe they don't complain about being controlled, provided that the control is absolute. Control, yes, what should I have said?

"Yes, Mister... Father, but w-what I was struggling with is, and I remember now," I said, finally, "it will destroy my life."

"Oh, no, the thing won't *kill* you. As you say, it loves you. It is in love with your soul, as much, or in the same way, as any animal loves its oppressor."

"It needs me, so it won't kill me, but it's giving me only one choice, or it *will* destroy the lives of innocents."

He again looked as if he felt sorry for me, like he was apologizing for something he felt he didn't do.

I needed to tell him, so I said, "And if I do that one thing it demands. It will destroy my life without ever needing to kill me. That's why I needed to see you."

"See a psychiatrist. I know a good one, but I cannot help you. Maybe you are not crazy, but also, maybe medication won't hurt."

At that point, the priest merely sat back, scrutinizing me, again smiling faintly when he should not have been smiling at all.

I heard it then, softly.

"Genau," I said.

"What was that?" he asked.

"What does the word mean? Does it sound familiar?"

"It's a German word. It is a way of saying 'this is exactly what I thought all along.'"

"That is what the thing said, just now. I think after the streets and the noise of the traffic, I must be in love too. That must be it."

IV. Fresh Flower Vending Machine

Some girls were taken up to heaven to be taught kissing by the angels, it seems, and then set back down to Earth to practice the art on their own. My first real kiss, not the one from fourth grade, when a chubby girl with frizzy hair and glasses snatched a kiss from my lips before leaving the classroom for the day, but the one that made my heart feel like it was escaping from my chest and made my eyes go dim, was the one I was always trying to recreate in someone else.

There must have been another experience like that out there, but I hadn't found it, though there was other kissing. Life may be a matter of trying, with all our hearts, to repeat the happiest moments and to try to fix those that are the most tragic by reliving those too, but in a way that repairs life and makes it all right. My first taste of love is what I wanted most to recapture, maybe for the rest of my life. Not the everything, but just the feeling, that thrill of standing at the edge of a thousand-foot cliff overlooking the ocean with the wind in my face.

That first time for me began downtown at The Lotus Lounge, several blocks from the college. I had a one-room, off-campus apartment there for a while. I was nineteen, trying school a second time, taking my required courses. I thought it would be an adventure to try living away from home, even if that were only a mile away. That little place was a blur of boredom, but I went back home to Dad's for most of my meals and laundry.

When I saw that I was likely failing in school again, I needed to have a few drinks, to take my mind off that feeling, to meet anyone who was into meeting. There are several bars and a couple of clubs on East Main. I first went to McLoughlin's where the "New Year's Eve and A Half Party" was in full swing—shoulder-to-shoulder crowded, a lot of pushing, and college football guys yelling. I was almost knocked to the floor more than once. The bartender felt bad for me, so he gave me a free drink, but I gave him a tip anyway.

It meant I still had enough cash in my pocket to go elsewhere. I tried The Lotus, which was almost next door, and it was the only bar on the strip with large windows and a bright enough interior that I could see what I was walking into. It looked quiet, a place for a quiet time.

It was at the Lotus Lounge that I saw the Latin girl, wearing a pink halter with a choker top, a white flower in her hair, and a short, green skirt with a palm leaf pattern on it that barely covered her thighs. She was talking and laughing with a friend, who was distractedly looking around the bar while talking to her. The girl with the flower turned to the door when I first walked in, but then she quickly turned back. After I walked to the bar, she looked over her shoulder at me again, this time with a smile, while I ordered a Jack and Coke.

I wasn't sure, but I thought I recognized her as the same girl who waved to me from the deli across the street a few days earlier, her hand wiggling in a little-girl wobble from outside. Her hair was bleached blonde, and she had it pinned up the first time I saw her, if it was her, but that night, it was down and to her shoulders, and she had a blood-red streak dyed on the left side. Her complexion was dark, and eyebrows were black. I preferred natural blondes, but the whole exotic look was nice for her.

After a minute, the friend, who was also wearing a short skirt, walked away to sit at a booth with a man, who was also alone, and the bleached blonde girl continued to look back and forth between me and her drink. She flung her hair back behind her shoulder and, after I was almost finished with my second drink, I walked over to her.

"Hey," I said. "You want to hear a joke?"

"Okay," she said, grinning.

"Are your parents bakers?"

"No. Why?"

"Because they sure made a cutie pie."

She looked at me blankly.

"You got it, right?"

"Yes. I think I heard that one before," she said with an obvious Spanish accent.

"Oh, sorry. It's a good one."

She nodded, smiling. "You are sweet."

"Aww. I'm Vinny. You are from?"

She laughed, covering her mouth. "Here."

I started to rattle the ice in my drink, as I tend to do when I'm nervous.

"You have an accent. So, I mean, where originally?"

"Oh, I come from Columbia."

"Cool! I've been trying to learn some Spanish. You must be here for work?" I asked.

She giggled again and nodded.

She smelled like roses, but also sweetly spicy from the flower in her hair.

"Oh, you're a bartender?"

She laughed outright, a bit loudly, then looked down and let her hair fall in front of her face.

"No, I don't work for Lotus bar, but the manager is very nice," she said, nodding. She was fidgeting on the stool.

"That's a gardenia, right?" I pointed at the blossom on the side of her head.

"Yes, I think."

"It is. If there are two things I know about, it's flowers and the local wildlife, thanks to my mom and dad."

She began then to tinker with the gardenia with both hands, and then I saw that she had taken it out.

"Then you go out to party a lot?" she asked.

I laughed, but I was careful that she wouldn't think I was laughing at her. "You mean the wildlife? No! I mean real wildlife. When I was a little boy, my dad used to take me out into the woods a lot."

She showed me the cut end of the stem. "It is in a little plastic vase for water, so it don't die!"

"Wow! That's very neat."

She handed it to me, and I put it to my nose. Closer, the gardenia had more of the syrupy smell of decay that gardenias get when they're a few days old. I tried to pin it back in for her but dropped it on the floor. I crouched down to pick it up and I couldn't help but see up her skirt. I couldn't see anything, though. It was too dark.

"I'm sorry," I said, handing the gardenia to her. "It lost some petals. It's my fault."

"Oh, no worry," she said. "Now is time I should go home."

"We just started talking."

She tossed the flower, along with its tiny capsule, over the bar and made it into the wastebasket on the other side. The bartender gave her a thumbs up.

"Well, you *are* very pretty," I added.

She looked at me in the eye in what my mom used to call a "come hither" look and then bit her lower lip for a second.

"Thank you. I'm glad you like."

"I like a lot," I said, conscious that I was smiling widely and a bit wolfishly. I was trying not to look too innocent. That might put her off if she was the type who wanted a man to make the first move.

She leaned forward on her stool and cocked her head toward me, then said under her breath, "Sweetie, do you mix business with pleasure?"

I didn't know what she was getting at, but she was talking, and I was listening, so it was a good start.

"I suppose I do," I said. "I like to have some fun when I work."

She laughed, a high-pitched giggle that was irresistible. "I have a problem at the end of my foot," she said in a serious tone and showed me where her toes were a little red and swollen, as if she were getting an infection.

"Wow, I'm sorry," I said. "It looks like it hurts."

"Oh, yes, very much," she said, then tsked. She shrugged and shook her head. "I have no insurance here, and it needs medicine for that."

"That's rough. I can help if you need that. I mean if it's not too much."

"Two hundred for doctor and prescription."

I whistled. I was working at a doughnut shop part-time while I was going to school and my dad would send me money when I was in a pinch, so I had some saved, but that was a lot to give to a stranger.

"Well, I'll tell you what; if you show me your place, then I'll stop at that ATM, and we'll have a deal."

I winked.

"Oh, I will take you there. My roommate is out tonight. She is there," she said, pointing to the girl she was talking with earlier. "She won't be back 'til the morning."

We walked the six or seven blocks to her apartment upstairs over a liquor store, and I got money out of the ATM around the corner from the bars. On the way, she told me that her name was Margarita, like the cocktail, but other than that, she didn't talk much. The apartment was more or less one big room with a loft for a bedroom with a ladder leading up to it. A little kitchenette was under the loft with a table and two chairs, and a door to the bathroom was next to that. I sat down on the couch and waited for her to sit down.

"Oh, no, we go up to the bed," she said, taking my wrist and tugging on it.

I thought maybe my lecher bit was too much. I wanted to talk and get to know her better.

"I want to hear about what it's like in Colombia and how you ended up here."

"No time for that," she said, leading me up the ladder.

"Don't hurt your foot," I said.

"It will be okay," she said, almost pulling me up.

She immediately began taking off her sandals and then unsnapped the collar from her top.

"Get your clothes off," she said, bare-breasted and undoing her skirt.

I sat on the bed and took everything off except my underwear.

"All your clothes," she said.

"Are you sure your roommate isn't coming in?"

"No. Is good. Lay down."

I lay down next to her, not sure if I should get under the covers or not, but it was warm even with the air conditioning, so I stayed on top.

She flipped the ceiling light off, which left the orange glow of a tulip-shaped lamp next to the bed, and then she lay next to me and threw her arm across me. It felt good, and I stroked it gently.

I was half in panic and half in tremulous excitement that moment with Margarita. We lay atop the thick, downy comforter, baby blue and dusty pink irises, with her head on my chest, as I inhaled her perfume on the back of her neck. I could smell that fruity, rose scent again that I remembered getting when I got close to her at the bar. She looked up at me smiling. I kissed her forehead. Her hair was smooth and shining in the light, but her eyes were nearly black, so I could barely see her pupils. I counted the flowers dancing in a rhythmic pattern on the wallpaper border looking up toward the ceiling as she traced small circles on my chest.

"If you want to kiss, that is okay," she said.

"Do you know this? It's something I memorized."

Margarita looked at me, puzzled.

"*This love that thou hast shown*
Doth add more grief to too much of mine own
Love is a smoke raised with the fume of sighs;
Being purged, a fire sparkling in lovers' eyes;
Being vexed, a sea nourished with loving tears.
What is it else? A madness most discreet,
A choking gall, and a preserving sweet."

"You are furry," she said.

"That was Shakespeare," I said, and laughed a bit.

"What is funny?" she asked.

"Never mind."

"Why?"

"You have no furry men in Columbia?"

"No so much," she said.

"You like it?"

"Yes. Is soft."

"So, I can kiss you?" I whispered into her ear.

"You can do that. Okay," she said looking a bit away, not looking too easy.

"Bring your lips to me," I said.

Her lips brushed mine, ever so lightly, like the wings of a butterfly, and then I kissed her fully. When I kissed that girl then, I would put aside those souvenirs from my teenage years. There were now grown-up games to play. I put the stained and broken toys away, and never looked at them again, because it all changed.

"You have bad breath," she said.

I was embarrassed, but I laughed. "Sorry, I would have brought gum. I didn't expect to kiss anyone tonight."

"Don't forget when you leave."

"Forget what? To brush my teeth?"

She furrowed her brow and looked disappointed for the first time. "My foot medicine, what we talk about."

"Oh, right. I got it. I won't forget you."

I wrapped my arms around her shoulders and squeezed her, pulling her face closer to mine.

"You are so cute boy," Margarita said, putting my hair behind my ears. "So cute little ears."

"People always notice my ears and big eyes." I'm sure I blushed because my face felt hot. "I must get them from my father."

"And nice big cock, too," Margarita said smiling, as she reached out and grasped it. "I like it."

That startled me and I gasped a bit. It was the first time someone else had touched my wiener. No, not the first time, really, but the first time as a man in a fully grown place. The first time I came was when I was twelve, during a dream. At first, I thought something was wrong with me and I was going to die; white thick fluid should not come out of my pee hole, but I was okay, no damage. It did feel good to touch it and rub it, and I learned that it was okay. It was normal, yet I was afraid I did it too often. There had to be a hidden problem with *that*.

"Wow," I said. "Um, what do you want to do with it?"

She put her nose to it and then brushed it with her tongue. I jumped a bit.

"Very clean too," she said and then looked to me with a smile. "Good."

"I'm always very clean," I said.

She immediately gave me my first blowjob, but again, not my first, but the first I felt was only for me, to make *me* feel good. My legs convulsed.

She stopped for a second to say, "Don't be so nervous. I'm not gonna hurt you!"

"It feels good, don't worry."

"Don't cum!" she said. "You have rubbers?"

"No." I said. "I wasn't expecting to be having sex tonight either!"

I honestly had never put one on before, and so I never thought of carrying them with me.

"Okay, then I won't let you fuck me, but you can use your fingers or mouth on me."

She then flipped her leg over my body, exposing her bottom to my face. I got more of that rose scent. It must have been there that she sprayed herself.

I tasted the lips of her opening. I never had done that before, and it made me very hard. I didn't want to cum already and ruin it for us. I started talking while darting my tongue across her labia, which sounds technical, but I don't like to be crude. It wasn't a crude moment for me.

"I fall in love easy, just a warning. I know this. I get big crushes sometimes, even at first sight. Sometimes it's romantic. Sometimes, it's that I see them like family, you know?"

"That is like Latin men," she said stopping for a few seconds. "Maybe you are part Latino."

"That's possible, for all I know."

"Don't fall in love with *me*."

"What if I do?"

"I don't want that."

"Okay, okay," I said.

As soon as she returned to licking and sucking me, I came. I tried to warn her, but I wasn't expecting it myself.

She said nothing, but got off the top of me, then quickly went down the ladder, naked and barefooted, to the bathroom. I heard water running.

When she came out, she yelled up to me. "You have money? My foot is bad!"

She climbed the ladder back up, and after we had our clothes on, I counted out the $200 in twenties.

"Okay, I need to sleep now," Margarita said flatly. "I almost forget about work in the morning."

"You work? Where?"

"At a store, at a store," she said. "Long day tomorrow."

"You didn't mention work on the way over."

After she put the money in her purse, I climbed down to the living area. She followed behind me and almost physically pushed me out the door.

On my way home I realized that I hadn't gotten her number or last name, but I knew where she lived, so felt it was okay to stop by again, though I'd felt I should wait a few days so I wouldn't look too pushy.

***

October, about a month ago, I thought about that night with Margarita. I wasn't clear on details with my disorganized memory by then, but I knew I must have been thinking about it, because it always triggered thoughts of Bernadette since we parted ways. I felt like I'd been cheating on her, but that night was the last clear, complete memory I had—the last one that was vivid, that I could smell and hear clearly. I thought I'd pay Bernadette a visit with a gift or card to lift her spirits while she was stuck in the hospital having her tests and treatments, because it was my fault she was in pain and going through what she was going through.

By then, I had to focus on every step when I walked, looking down to see where each foot was planted. The hospital was only six blocks away though, so I made it there without a problem. In the lobby, right across from the double entrance doors, my eyes caught a lime green vending machine that dispensed bouquets of flowers—a choice of carnations, roses, or a mix of daisies—*Oh, Daisy! Oh, my God, Daisy!*—and in various sizes in cut glass vases. They were displayed on revolving shelves behind glass windows, no different than a choice of slices of pie in the automat machines that I had seen in pictures from decades ago. I approached the machine, almost mesmerized by its shiny newness, and simplicity. It made a difficult decision much easier to make, and so I took a $20 bill out of my wallet to get the large bouquet of roses.

A plump woman, who was about sixty, with white hair and eyeglasses attached to a chain around her neck was sitting behind a counter watching me while I tried to focus on getting the $20 bill to go into the slot about a dozen times. I glanced over to her, and I couldn't tell whether she was amused or suspicious, but she was looking up and down between her desk and me, which made me uncomfortable.

"Sir? Do you need *help* with something?" she asked, a little too loudly to be courteous.

"Thank you, I'll get it," I said.

After two more attempts, the machine took the money, and I pushed the button. The shelf turned around, but then the door didn't open. I tugged at it a few times.

"If you need help, I can call someone!" the woman shouted across the lobby as she began getting up from her seat.

"No, no, it's all right," I said.

The woman looked back and forth across the hospital lobby, and then down the corridor behind me, before picking up the phone.

I left right then and watched my feet while walking back home so I wouldn't trip.

V. Those We Say We Love

Bernadette was wearing latex cleaning gloves when she took a pack of cigarettes and an ashtray from the junk drawer by the stove. She pulled a cigarette out of the pack and lit it.

"You're smoking again," I said, a bit alarmed. "You haven't smoked since we got married."

"Nope. Before that. I quit when I got pregnant," she said, the cigarette in the corner of her mouth.

"Oh," I said, "well, it's not good for you."

"I'm aware. I only smoke when I really need it."

"Oh, okay," I said. "You'll burn the glove."

"Are you my mother? I'm only taking a few drags."

"Oh, okay," I said.

"I found some more books that're yours. I packed 'em in a box next to the fridge."

Bernadette double-knocked the side of the box with her foot. "Not anything good, I suppose, or you would've missed them."

"I don't know what I got yet. I don't have all my stuff out of the boxes at Alex's place," I said.

Bernadette asked me to leave the apartment just before she filed for divorce. I was blindsided by it, but with everything that had happened, I suppose I shouldn't have been. I had to question why it happened when it did, though. We lost so much and had grief to share, but I suppose it was also grief that ended it, because it was bigger than the love, at least for Bernadette. I knew that; I'd always known that, but I failed as a student, in making a good career, so what was there for her to hang on to? For almost three years between the divorce and Dad's accident that led me to move back home, I lived in a small upstairs apartment of bare wires and two-by-fours with a guy who'd been in college probably forever.

I could just barely afford the place, even sharing rent, because I wasn't able to keep a job for more than a few months without losing it. Either I worked too slowly or wandered off too much. I was homeless for the first few days after I left. I'd hang out at the bus station or Food Mart at night. Though I didn't tell her, Bernadette knew. She'd let me come back to the apartment long enough to shower and change clothes. Most of the day, I hung out at the college campus, and there I found an ad in the college newspaper looking for a roommate. Alex was a tall, brawny guy with a little goat's beard—he looked like a football player, but I doubt he ever played. He didn't have that kind of spirit. There were too many I's in his team, though he wasn't ashamed to use others when he needed to.

"Hm, okay. Alex? That's the guy's name?"

"Yeah."

"Does he seem like a good guy?"

"He can be when he wants to be."

"Hm, well, that's good."

"If he lays off the Stroh's." I chuckled a bit.

"It's been a few months. It's about time you settled in there."

"It's not a big apartment like this one. The whole place is about as big as our living room."

Bernadette propped her arms behind herself on the counter and sighed, then she turned and crushed the cigarette out, and put the pack and ashtray away. "So, anyway, I'm sure you have things to do."

"Nothing important. Where were they?" I asked.

"What?"

"The books."

"Under the couch, which was weird. I was moving the furniture—putting the couch under the window, you know, so I'm not looking into the sun when I'm watching TV."

I walked over to the box, and she began pulling on the ends of the fingers of her gloves. "I don't know why you had that many books under the couch," she said with that harshness rising in her voice.

I opened the flaps and looked at a few of them.

"Come on, Vinny. Don't take them all out again."

"I'm not. I'll put them back."

I looked over the second layer of books and placed them carefully on the table.

"Oh, wow, yeah. My first edition of *One Hundred Years of Solitude*, with the original dust jacket." I began putting the others back into the box. "I could get a couple of hundred dollars for it if I sold it."

"Why don't you? You just got fired. You could use the money," she said, taking the gloves off and laying them on the table next to the box.

"I haven't read it yet."

"Sell that one and buy a cheap paperback to read."

"I have an interview with a security company tomorrow. I think I'll probably get it."

I put the books back into the box, closed it up, and then bent over to pick it up.

Once I had a grip on the box I almost fell forward, dropping it.

"Jesus Christ, Vinny," she said.

"It was heavier than I thought it was," I said with a little laugh.

"You need to work out. You've got that valuable book in there."

"It's on the top; it'll be fine."

"You can't pack that many in one box."

"*You* packed them," I said, laughing again.

"I have a headache," she said.

It *was* heavy and overfilled. I carried it down the stairs, then pushed the door open with my back.

After putting the box in the back seat, I went back up to the apartment, but Bernadette had locked the door. I knocked.

She shouted from inside. "Vinny?"

"Yes!"

"Did you forget something?"

"I thought I'd visit a little since I was here."

"I have a headache!"

"Are you going to unlock the door?"

I heard the creaky spring in the sofa inside.

"Jesus Christ, Vinny," Bernadette said unlocking the bolt, and then opened the door.

"If it's a bad time, I can go," I said.

"Of course, it's a bad time. I told you I have a headache."

"I can get you something."

"I have aspirins."

Bernadette turned away, walked sluggishly into the living room and slumped onto the overstuffed chair.

"I don't really have a headache, okay? I just need rest," she said.

"Aren't you sleeping all right?"

"Yes!"

I sat on the sofa, then looked at her and smiled. She had her head tipped back, and her eyes were closed. Her lips were so red, even without lipstick. She opened one eye to look at me.

"Vinny," she asked, "what do you want?"

"While I was putting pictures away this morning, I was thinking about when we met."

"Why?" she said, closing her eye again.

"I don't know why I think things. I don't have control over it." I laughed, but Bernadette didn't move.

After a minute, she said, "We know how we met. Why do you want to talk about it?"

"You told me once how your parents met, and it was a nice story. I think it would be nice now to think about some happy times from the past."

"We were drunk. I was a friend of Angie's, and you worked with her," she said, lifting her head up and opening her eyes.

"Angie from the Safeway deli, yeah. I haven't seen her in a long time. I wonder if she has the same number."

"She doesn't."

"How do you know?" I asked, laughing again.

"We still talk. She and her new boyfriend were here just a few nights ago," she said, looking me in the eye. "I knew her before I even met you. We used to sneak out together at night and drink vodka and orange juice in the park when we were in high school."

"Oh, yeah," I said. "She fixed us up, right?"

"Yeah," she said, sitting forward, "because she said you needed to get laid."

I laughed again.

"That's all it was supposed to be," she said. "We were drunk, and we had sex. You weren't good at it."

"But you saw me again, so it couldn't have been too bad."

"Only because I thought you were cute, and you made me feel needed."

I smiled at her. "I'm good at that," I said. "You were going through a rough time then, and I was happy I could help you out."

Bernadette shifted in the seat, then sat straight up, pushing her chest up and her chin out, as if she were daring me to take a swipe at her. She even put her fists up and placed them against her breasts.

"No, you don't understand. You made *me* feel needed because you needed someone to take care of *you*!"

I looked down at my feet, not sure at first what to say.

She relaxed her posture a bit, but the tension in her body shifted to her voice. "You needed a mommy, and I wanted to be one."

"Well, that's—that's not really true."

"It fucking *is* true! You were a sweet, cute guy. I don't see that much around here—so I fell for you for a little while, yes—but you can't wipe your own goddam ass!"

I fixed my eyes to the floor then. I wasn't sure what had brought that on. I sat in silence for a minute. "Hey, ba—"

"Then I found out I was pregnant! Oh my God, fuck!" She stood up at that point. "Do you understand what my dilemma was now?"

Still, I kept my eyes fixed on the floor, my shoes. Whatever happened I didn't want to look her in the eye. I wasn't there to challenge her. "You don't have to fight about it now."

Bernadette began to pace the room. I would only look at my own feet.

She walked away to the other side of the living room, and then turned around to face me. "Is there anything else you want to know, Vinny? I mean, as long as you're here?"

"I guess not," I said.

"Good! I'm sure I've said it before."

"So, that's all for now then," I said, not knowing on which spot my eyes should rest. "I just thought we could talk."

Her face grew red. "No, we can't talk! I don't *want* to talk! I want my life now! I want whatever the hell life I was supposed to have before it went to shit!"

I didn't know what I should say, so I just started for the door. When I got to it, I turned around. I almost mumbled. "You don't have to be mad at me forever."

She charged at me, just a few steps. "About what? I don't have to get mad about what?"

"I-I don't—never mind."

She reached across me and threw the door open, almost hitting me with it.

"Get the fuck out! Get the FUCK OUT!" she yelled, trembling.

I started out the doorway, then stopped to look at her, but not in the eye—her jeans, maybe.

She sucked in air between her teeth, her body very rigid.

"I care about you, but I can't do this again, not for a while," she said.

"I don't know what I'm going to do," I said.

"Go!" Her voice cracked. Her eyes were tearing up.

"Never mind," I said, turning around to face the door and stairs.

"OUT! OUT! OUT! OUT! OUT! OUT!" she repeated until she started to lose her voice altogether.

I started down the stairs.

Bernadette slammed the door with such force that a piece of the molding over the door frame came loose and hung, swinging.

When I was almost to the bottom, I turned around again and looked up.

I said, not loud enough for her to hear, because it didn't matter, "What did I do?"

I tried not to cry.

"What did I do?" I asked softly again.

All the way from the downstairs entrance door, I could hear her sobbing. I never heard her cry like that. She always had the stiff upper lip.

"What did I do?"

I could still hear her crying in wails, even from the car.

She screamed, "You knew she was fascinated with stairs! Why did you open that basement door, motherfucker!"

***

Except for bumping into her once the following February when I was picking up Chinese food, the next time we were able to talk for long was over two years later, because I didn't dare call her, and she didn't call me, except when Dad died. We didn't get together then, because we didn't have a funeral for Dad, or even a memorial, and so she felt there was no point. When she called, she said she always sensed that there might have been some bad blood between me and Dad, though it was obvious that I loved him despite it, and she was right on both counts. It was Bernadette who wanted Dad and me to spend some time together— "father-son time"—the day that everything happened, but I wanted her and Abby to come too, so we could all be together for once. Otherwise, we might never have been there at all.

When I finally had the nerve to call her, it was to ask if she'd pick up the red foil box I found after I moved back home, and I was surprised that she was agreeable to coming over.

"It would be nice to see you, I suppose," she said, though she wasn't going to see the real me, but a perverted composite drawing of me and the thing. Still, she said she thought it would be nice.

When she got to the house, I had the red box sitting on the kitchen table for her, just in case.

"Wow. You look like shit. I thought I looked bad lately," she said.

"Yeah, sorry."

Bernadette was right; she didn't look much better. She was pale with dark circles around her eyes—beaten or defeated—like I'd never seen her before.

"Did you see my mother at all in the last few months?"

"The Fourth of July—no, the day after. I wanted to see how she was getting along."

"Did she want to see you?"

"Not really, no, but she wasn't in the mood to talk much. She kept getting this deep pain in her hip. She'd clench her teeth and grab the arm of the chair each time it came back, and it did a few times while I was there. I told her to go to a doctor, but she told me I should leave."

Bernadette closed her eyes and nodded. "That started in June sometime," she said. "Mother always says doctors might make the sick feel better, but people only die after they've seen one, so she'd never go." Bernadette rolled her eyes. "Not for an illness anyway." She started massaging her temples. "Instead of making an appointment, she started to take aspirin and Tylenol like it was candy, but when they stopped working, she couldn't sleep at night, so she gave in."

"That was good. I'm glad she went."

"After looking at her, he ordered some scans and a biopsy."

"I knew about the pain, but I didn't know she went through all of that."

"It's bone cancer, or in the cartilage."

"Oh, wow," I said. Again, for a while, I couldn't look at her. "I tried calling her a few times a couple of weeks ago, but no one answered."

"They started her on radiation treatment right away—and morphine." Bernadette looked above my head at the unwashed dishes and scowled but continued. "She didn't want to see me either at first, but we're talking now. She did say she wanted you to stay away."

"I figured that out. I love her anyway. I can't help that."

Bernadette began to look through her purse and shook her head.

"What's Bruce doing?"

"I've been looking in on Dad and the VA is providing a nurse, but he's getting along better on his own."

"All right," I said.

After what seemed like an eternity, she added "I'm sorry."

Bernadette told me then about the agonizing head and neck pain she had been having herself and that I knew she'd have.

"It started about a week ago. On and off, but it's gotten worse since then."

"Are you taking something?"

"It's more than a headache. I don't know. After about three days of it, it moved to my neck too." She showed me with her finger where it started and traced a line to where it ended. "It feels like the back of my neck is being pressed in a vise, cutting off the blood to my head."

"You should see a doctor," I said.

"I did, just yesterday. He fucking barely looked at me. He dug his fingers into the back of my head and asked me if it hurt. 'Yes, it fucking hurts.' So, he said it's probably tension and stress after what happened, and then my mother getting sick. He might be right. We'll see."

"Didn't he do anything for it?"

"He gave me a prescription for ibuprofen and a muscle relaxer. I started them as soon as I got home yesterday, but they haven't done a damned thing."

She sighed and stared off across the kitchen for a few seconds before she snapped back from wherever her mind had wandered.

"Why are you sitting on the floor?" she asked. "It's filthy."

I recognized what her pain was, where it was coming from, and so I decided it was right to explain to her what had happened, because she thought I no longer had feelings for her.

"Is this the box of her stuff?" she asked, putting her hand on the red box.

"Yeah," I said, "I need to tell you something." I tried to put words together, but under stress, it was even more difficult.

After I gave myself a minute to collect my thoughts, I confessed it all. I told her about the night in the woodlot, about seeing the thing, how it came into me, and about what it demanded—all of it, in detail.

"Jesus, Vinny, that's really fucked up. I mean... I'm sure it was a joke," she said, walking toward the back door from the kitchen, not even looking at me. "Someone made it up to spook you; you're so damned gullible and superstitious."

"No one told me anything," I said to the floor tiles. "I-I was alone. I didn't even tell Alex about it after I got home, even though it was there with us." The words were difficult, but I persisted. "He would laugh in my face, if I did."

She glanced back at me as if she were afraid, or worried, as if I would chase her if she ran, but then she began to slowly shake her head, almost imperceptibly.

"No one *needs* to tell me anything. It tells me things itself," I said with effort, feeling that I would cry if I could.

After rubbing her shoulder for a minute, she sighed again deeply. "I don't know," and then picked up a pizza box and some napkins from the floor. She stuffed them into the garbage can. "Jesus Christ, get a grip on the house. You'll have rats if you don't already have them."

"Wait," I said, "This is important."

"I have to go. I don't have time for this," she said, looking to the door.

"Just one thing."

"Like the doctor told *me*, it's stress. It's due to the thing with your dad, especially after Abby. You've got a lot on your emotional plate."

"I wondered what animals thought, how they think, and what pictures they have in their heads. I think I know now because the thing is inside me."

"Oh my God, Vinny, I really need to go." she said, picking up Dad's box, and then opening the screen door.

"It's feeding off people I love and transferring that energy to me."

"You need help," she said, looking at me steadily in the eyes for the first time in months.

"Yeah. Yeah, you're right, but there is no help."

"There are numbers you can call," she said.

"I talked to a priest and he told me to see a shrink. A shrink isn't going to get rid of it."

Bernadette took a step out the doorway, then back in, then out, and back in again.

"It's why you're having the pain." I added, "It's a curse."

I sensed she was afraid, fighting against herself to stay put.

"All right," I said, finally.

"I'll call you when I get home if I'm feeling better. My head is starting to kill me again."

"It won't... get better, or kill you either. I wish I could do something."

A few days later, she did call from the hospital. Stabbing pains began to attack her shoulders; they felt like someone plunging a knife into her, over and over. It had gotten so bad after a while that she had trouble eating, and what little she could eat, she would throw up. She went to the emergency room, and the doctor there was concerned about her weight loss and that she was clearly in agony, and so he immediately admitted her to the hospital.

VI. Reverie

Sycamores with their sick, white limbs like lepers, stood in a meandering line on the other side of the street. The trees were almost identical, but there were no houses on that side for another two blocks either way. On the far side of the trees was a cyclone fence to keep kids from drowning in a narrow but deep stream that ran back there, and beyond that there was a stretch of wetlands.

The sycamore trees were no taller than when I was a boy. Do they stop growing at a certain age? I felt, when I moved back home this year, after Dad died, as if I were so much older than twenty-six, because it felt like so many years had flown by, like the individual pages for each day of a wall calendar that fly off in old movies to show the passage of time.

Few things had changed on the street I grew up on. The colors of the other houses were the same as before. A couple of them had been painted in the years since we moved in, but they were repainted the same colors. Our house, where I grew into me, and where I would have another life again once Mom and Dad were gone, was white, even the trim—Dad's "white elephant"—a small, Craftsman house with a narrow porch across the front that looked out onto the street. It was refreshing to sit out on it, like I did that day, without the sun shining in on us most of the year, like it did in the back of the house, streaming dusty rays through the kitchen window.

We didn't talk with the neighbors when we first moved in that I can remember—I was very young—but as time went on, they would say hello or chat with Mom and Dad in the front yard. The family to the right of us, a man and his wife whose elderly mother lived with them, kept a rabbit in a mesh cage behind their garage. They also had a daughter, but she was at college while I was still little. I'd seen her, maybe twice. She was a contestant on a TV gameshow once, and she did some modelling for a car show. I remember seeing her on their front lawn in a yellow crepe gown. Maybe she'd been a bridesmaid at a wedding that day, but to me, it was as if she were a movie actress winning an award. She waved to me that morning, in the slanted, orange sunshine, while I left for school. The couple talked to Mom and Dad four or five times, maybe, and I played with the rabbit once.

The elderly woman in the house to the left of us spoke halting English with a German accent. She walked with her arms folded across her chest as if they were a cradle for her shriveled breasts. I'd never seen her smile. "Mrs. Greta," I called her, though I imagine that was her first name. I don't know if I had ever met a "Mr. Greta," if he were alive when we moved in. She brought us leftover butterscotch pudding from her church's picnic one time, but Mom threw it out because it was "bad."

I'd seen the old woman engaged in short conversations with Mom a few times over the boxwoods, usually about her health problems, once about a surgery she was scheduled to have on her neck, while I watched them from the porch. She scowled when she spoke, as if something in her mouth tasted bad and she was repeatedly shaking her head and pulling her hair into place.

As the years passed, one of Mrs. Greta's sons and his wife would come over to mow the lawn, shovel the occasional snow, or just check in on her. The son's daughter had a baby girl the day before Bernadette had Abby and they were in the maternity ward together. When she got older, Dad watched the girl sometimes, because the son's wife was the ambulance dispatcher for a while, and she trusted Dad. He let her play in the yard and use my swing set when she was old enough. She even had permission to come over for snacks a few times.

There was one house on the street that I'd never seen anyone go in or out of, but a light was on at night at least once or twice. I called it "the mystery house." There were plants in the windows, so someone was watering them, and their lawn was mowed too, though not often, but in all these years, I never caught anyone mowing it. I often thought about the mystery people and where they might be and what they might do. I imagined that the owners were elderly and retired. People who had nowhere to go, but they probably would be dead by now, and it still looks the same years later. I thought sometimes that maybe they needed someone to visit them, or maybe they *didn't* want anyone to visit them, and that was why they never went out.

I felt certain the other houses on the street were prettier inside than the "white elephant" was, like houses in soap operas, decorated with French furniture and those fancy gold-framed portrait paintings. I went to a classmate's house for a cast party in high school when I worked on the stage crew of the spring musical. It wasn't something I was much interested in, but it would be a way to make friends. Our English teacher with the British accent, was the director and brought her husband with her. He wore oil-stained jeans, like he was working under a car, and he smelled like a brewery; not what I ever expected for the husband of a teacher. That singing kid lived on a street five or six blocks away. The house was beautiful inside, and they had just that kind of furniture, like in *As the World Turns*.

Before I started middle school, I'd been in and out of a few of the other kids' houses when Dad tried to get me into Boy Scouts. I needed his help with some of the projects, but with his working different hours from one week to the next, it wasn't easy, so we pulled out of it, but even then, I hadn't seen the inside of one house on *this* street. No one had children my age that I'd ever seen or heard. No kids with whatever noises they would make. There were only the adult sounds of power tools, revving engines, whirring trimmers, my noisy bike, and someone had a rooster somewhere not far away.

***

After Mom died, we didn't talk to the neighbors again that I remember. Dad was even less sociable than he had been before. He never approached anyone unless he had a plan prepared for them in his head. The neighbors stopped saying even "how ya doing?" when we stepped outside like they sometimes did before. After Dad died, and I moved back into the house, I'd barely seen the neighbors more than a few times. The street had become silent and lifeless. At most, there were the chirping of grasshoppers and whistle of the wind through the trees. People pulled in and out of driveways and there was occasional yard work, but no one ever spoke to me. No one smiled and waved, and except for the mail lady, no one ever came up to the door, as if our house were abandoned, and as if I were never here at all.

I sat on our porch swing that afternoon, staring out at that line of lepers, like I did when I was a boy. I next got it into my head, whenever that might have been, that nothing inside or outside was *our* anything anymore, but mine, not even my three-year wife's, but mine. The lepers were reaching out to each other, as a dry breeze blew. They were probably lonely, rooted into the ground, unable to move, but who would want to love them and their grisly, gray trunks? They make music at times when the wind is strong enough, but in the highest of summer their music is weak on the best of days, and that day the trees and the white line of the street were out of focus. Maybe I might've needed glasses. Dad did, and his eyes only got worse over time. Maybe it was the thing that had made everything else different.

I had trouble making the best choices for myself, even before. My decisions drifted up like fluffy clouds as I made them, but they predictably rained down later, because I based them on my feelings over facts, but I'd trust my feelings the next time just as much, and I stood by them. Dad said that the only times I was ever stubborn and stood my ground was when I was wrong, and I suppose that's true. Few concrete things drew my attention—I'd walk into walls if I wasn't paying attention—but pure emotion, the instinct of the moment, my internal values, those I understood.

I picked up some of that jargon in a psychology book somewhere, but it described me. I could instinctively sense what was true and what was false, or I could, I think, before the change. After that, decisions just happened to me, and I shadowed them. I lived in a colorful inner world of emotion, in whatever made me happy, because what was *outer* rarely did. I'd prefer the external world to mirror my personal beliefs. I wanted to live a life as true to myself as possible, but that was uncertain now.

All my senses together, as a whole, had dulled twice as much by halfway into this summer, as if I were at the bottom of the deep end of a swimming pool, and yet each particular sense, individually, was sharper. It was if the thing were allowing me full control of one sense at a time, so I could better focus on the environment around me. I could smell intensely but not hear, or see sharply and clearly, yet my body was numb, as if I only floated about a room. Each day during midsummer, I could hear more and smell more of those things that I wasn't accustomed to noticing. Others disappeared, as if they moved on to an unseen dimension. Birds were singing mating calls from the trees to bushes, and I stopped to listen.

I had been ready that day for work with nothing left but to put on my company cap. I did shower, but I was already starting to loathe the feel of the water, and the smell of the soap was too strong. I got up and went inside to where I left my cap but feeling no different than I had the previous few days. Like my parents had, I used the back door that led to the kitchen when going to the car, because it was closer to the driveway.

I locked it with the inside knob and then closed it behind me. There's one step down from the door, which I knew was there, but I stepped too far out, missing the step entirely, which caused me to trip and fall on my palms onto the gravel. When I stood up, my wrists were sore and my palms were red, throbbing, scratched here and there, but I was otherwise all right. I knew that step down was there since I was five, but for the first time, I missed it.

When I got to the car, I tried to fit the key into the door at least a dozen times, but it seemed impossibly small, as if I were threading a needle. I stepped back into the shade of the front yard and sat in the grass, breathing deeply and heavily, thinking it was the sun and heat, trying to refocus, rubbing my eyelids and temples.

After a few minutes, I went out again and tried several more times before giving up. I froze where I stood, staring at the car, trying to remember what I was even supposed to do to get it out of the driveway if I had gotten the door open. I finally went back to the porch and sat on the swing again. I stayed there until I realized I would be late for work unless I started right then to walk the nearly three miles. That was when I found I also couldn't cry tears.

VII. Gradus ad Parnassum

Over ancient Catania, snow-capped Etna stood ready to engulf the city in lava and ash at any moment. Along the shore, Gabriella Corsetti floated in a blue floral beach coverup. She was a scrawny girl of eighteen with a boyish frame, squinting chestnut eyes, and a bend in her nose. She let her black, curlicued hair grow long, but she kept it piled on the top of her head, tied up with white ribbons like Artemis on an urn. She was shoeless, bounding from rock to rock by the sunbaked coast, and there she met Lt. Bruce Brookes, a tall, blonde and blue-eyed American navy pilot who was stationed at Sigonella. He was nine years her senior and missing an incisor, the result of a fight with a drunken fisherman outside of *Le Quattro Spade* just the previous night.

Bruce was smoking a slim, brown cigar with a fellow officer on the seawall when he waved to her. Gabriella coyly waved back to him with one hand, and with the other, shaded her eyes from the sun.

"Hello!" she shouted.

"You know English?" Bruce shouted down to her, whistling on the word "English."

"Yes," she said. "I speak English very well, thank you."

"The water is rough there," Bruce shouted back. "If you fall in, you'll drown."

His friend laughed, nudging Bruce. "She is there every day!"

"I fell in many times, and I will again. I am sure!" said Gabriella. "I'm a good swimmer. Sometimes I dive from the cliff."

"Keep that up and you *will* die!"

"My brother dives with me. He knows the water!" she shouted, jutting out her chin.

Bruce moved to the edge of the wall, then gestured for the girl to come closer. "Why don't you come up here? The waves and seagulls are loud and talking is hard enough for me," he said pointing to his mouth and smiling.

"Did you win the fight?"

"I'd say I did. He crawled off whimpering." The lieutenant shrugged. "I felt bad for him."

The other officer shouted down to the girl on the rocks, "He was defending a damsel in distress! This man is a gentleman, and a genuine hero!"

"I don't meet heroes every day," Gabriella said from the edge of the grey wall.

Bruce raised his hands. "One hundred percent trustworthy. I'm a pilot!"

"My brothers tell me to stay away from the men at the base." Gabriella rolled her eyes. "But I was eighteen yesterday, so I will do as I please."

She reached her hands up to the handsome officer, who pulled her to the top of the wall and landed her gracefully down.

Letting go of her arms, Bruce then bowed to her. "Happy birthday, yesterday."

"I'm a Virgo, so you'd better mind your manners."

"He always does," said the other officer.

"You're so skinny," Bruce said laughing. "Doesn't your mama feed you?"

"Yes, and she is an excellent cook, but I get a lot of exercise."

The other officer laughed. "You have knees like doorknobs."

"You can say that," she said turning to him, "but I plan to be an elegant and graceful lady in my time."

"I'm sure you will be!" Bruce said and laughed as well.

***

When I first met Gabriella, she was pulling the skewers out of fruit at Bernadette's cousin Wendy's wedding reception and handing the berries and grapes to her husband in a paper bowl. Bernadette's dad was having trouble with the smaller finger foods. I knew no one there, except Bernadette, who was my girlfriend at the time, and the caterer's assistant, who was a Puerto Rican girl from my high school graduating class. What was her name? Marisol, I'll say. She said she thought she remembered me, and I chatted with her for a short time, but she was busy.

Bernadette and I hadn't been dating for much longer than a month, but I went to the reception with her as a date, because she didn't want to go alone, and we had important news that she wanted to break to her mom and dad. Bernadette thought that the reception was as good a place as any, because her parents wouldn't create a scene around the extended family, and she couldn't predict how they would react if she were alone with them.

After hearing only Bernadette's complaints of her "old-fashioned" mother, I pictured Gabriella as an Italian stereotype—loud and obese, with a mustache, stirring a pot of sauce, but she looked nothing like that. She was beautiful, not for her age, but for any age. The only clue that she was forty was that her hair was streaked with silver here and there, but in just the right places. It was set in a loose, coiled bun, like a cinnamon roll, at the nape of her long neck, with a gold pin or comb holding it in place.

Gabriella looked up, her eyes bright, and smiled broadly at me when she saw the two of us approaching, then she offered her hand, and I gallantly grasped her fingers, like I'd seen in movies. She had full lips and a soft, caring expression, unlike Bernadette who was thin-lipped, like her father. Bernadette's mouth was always set firmly closed like a purse, and with her piercing hazel eyes, and strong jaw, she looked defiant—a warrior priestess. Bernadette resembled her dad much more than her mom. While Bernadette was hometown pretty, her mom had an aura of glamour, like when you spot someone famous eating at a restaurant, but you can't quite place who it is.

Gabriella was wearing a form-fitting, wine-red sequined gown that showed off her narrow waist, with a small, cropped jacket with feathers on the shoulder that Bernadette told me was called a "bolero." Gabriella had a habit of shaking her finger at anyone she spoke to until she came to her point, when she would lay her hands in her lap, and turn the many rings she had on her fingers while listening.

She and Bruce sat in two chairs at the reception, placed along the wall of the VFW hall, which was cinder-block gray and dimly lit with Christmas lights and paper lanterns. Bruce, at the time, had just turned forty-nine but looked at least ten years older. He wore a dark grey suit and bow tie. The whites of his eyes were a bit yellowed, his eyebrows were overgrown, and his lower lip hung loose from his face. I extended my hand to him. He stared at it for a moment before loosely grasping it.

"We sh-should swim t-to the lighthouse!" he said, letting go of my hand.

Gabriella looked to him and then to me, losing her smile for a moment.

"Excuse him," she said.

Bernadette crossed in front of me and kissed his forehead. "He is still a little confused now and then."

Gabriella smiled at her husband. "He thinks one word, but another comes out at times, but he has been getting better with his therapy.

Bruce smiled to his wife and touched her hand.

"I did not see you at the wedding," Gabriella said, sitting forward.

"W-we were outside the church," I said.

"Why would you stay out?" she asked, looking at both of us, confused. "Wendy would have been happy to see you there."

Bernadette quickly moved to get two chairs from one of the tables to sit facing her parents to deliver the news and I followed.

"Mama, this is Vinny," Bernadette said, putting her hand on her mother's chair. "We have something to discuss."

"Lovely to meet you, Vinny," Gabriella said.

She took a deep breath and set her face into a steady and somber gaze.

"It's not bad," I said.

"But it *is* important, I see," said Gabriella.

Bernadette looked down at her lap for a second and took a breath. "I'm going to have a baby."

Gabriella frowned and then turned to Bruce to whisper something into his ear.

The voices of the others at the reception receded, muffled, into the background, though I could clearly hear the DJ playing "Brown-Eyed Girl."

Gabriella looked at her daughter as if she were a heretic. "You are always trouble. You know how I feel about such things."

My heart pounded in my chest.

Gabriella then glanced toward me and offered only a weak smile this time, while Bruce continued to carefully eat, and then she looked back toward Bernadette. After a while, she said, "Is this young man the father?"

"Yes, he is." Bernadette looked toward me. Her cheeks were turning pink.

"Please tell me that you will be married soon."

Bernadette again glanced toward me. She hesitated, swallowing. "Yes. That is the plan," she said.

Gabriella's smile came back, more broadly again, and then she firmly clasped Bernadette's hand and mine. "I know you have little time. It doesn't need to be a fancy wedding, as long as there is a marriage."

"With the short notice," Bernadette said with a shrug, "I guess we could plan a civil ceremony and have a bigger, church wedding after the baby is born."

Bernadette again looked to me with her brow furrowed.

"Nonsense!" said Gabriella, still holding our hands.

We didn't have time to plan a big event with people, when the baby was due in March.

I only said, "I suppose if—" before Gabriella cut me off.

"No! Nonsense about big weddings! All we care about is the paper! A loving mommy and daddy are what are important for a baby, not wedding dresses and cakes. We want no bastards in our family."

"We'll make the best of it," said Bernadette.

"There are too many broken families. Those are not healthy," Gabriella said, looking at me. "My husband and I have been married for twenty-one years, and we have been through so much heartbreak, and it was even harder this year after this stroke, but we have each other. We are like one."

Gabriella let go of our hands, and Bernadette sat back, taking a deep breath.

"You have your own money?" Gabriella asked me.

"Yes, I suppose I do," I said. "I work at the meat counter at Safeway." I hadn't yet started work at the warehouse.

"You are a butcher?"

"No, nothing like that. I don't think I could cut up animals. The meats are precut and prepackaged in boxes, and I only slice them or trim them sometimes."

Gabriella shrugged.

I continued. "And there's cheese too."

Gabriella folded her hands in her lap, silent for a moment. She tilted her head and smiled at me, giving my face a once-over. "You will give me adorable grandbabies, but you should not be working at a Safeway. I don't want my daughter to marry a tapeworm, but a grocery store is not a career."

I laughed. "I don't want to be a tapeworm. That would be pretty awful."

Bernadette again gave me a quick glance. "They do like him a lot there."

"I am sure they do." Gabriella reached out and patted me lightly on the cheek. "Dark hair, eyes, complexion... are you *Italian*?"

"Mama!" Bernadette said.

Once more Bernadette looked at me, this time narrowing her eyes. I wasn't sure what I was supposed to say, so I stayed close to the truth. I shrugged. "Well, I'm Irish and Swedish on my mother's side. She was a tall redhead."

"Our Bruce is part Irish too," Gabriella said with a wave of her hand. "And a few other things. He is a mutt." She smiled to him, then leaned over and kissed his cheek.

Bruce smiled to his wife and then returned to eating his fruit.

"I suppose I am, too, maybe," I said.

"And your father?"

"Um..."

Bernadette helped me. "Italian, yes." She then looked at me. "And a little Greek too, right?"

"I guess so, yeah." I said.

Gabriella reached out and took my face in her hands. "And so handsome. You look like a puppy." She looked to Bernadette. "Those big eyes. I just want to squeeze him."

I felt sick.

"Yes," said Bernadette. "He *is* a cute guy. He doesn't lack anything in the looks department."

Gabriella frowned to her daughter. "I don't know why you didn't leave your hair dark. It was beautiful."

"It's still beautiful," I said, smiling at Bernadette.

"I'll go back to the brown sometime, Mama."

Gabriella looked to me, putting her hand on my knee. "Look at your fiancée, she bleaches her hair."

I smiled to Gabriella, then to looked to Bernadette. "I don't plan to dye mine. It's staying black."

Gabriella laughed; it turned out that she was easier to be around than I thought. "You are a nice boy, Vincenzo. I see that!" she said shaking the finger. "You are a *gentiluomo*. You marry my daughter, so our grandbaby has a complete family, with a mother and father, just like it should be."

I looked to Bernadette and put my hand on her knee. "Well, I sure want to."

"Wedding!" Bruce said, looking up from his bowl.

"Yes," Gabriella said to him. "Wendy got married today!"

"Oh, I know," said Bruce, as if to prove to her nothing was wrong with his memory.

"Now, why did you stay out? You were invited and could bring a guest. It was beautiful!" Gabriella looked back and forth, between me and Bernadette, this time maybe a bit angrily.

"Vinny's been having car trouble, so we would have been late, and he didn't have anything dressy to wear anyway," Bernadette explained.

"Nonsense!" Gabriella said looking to me. "You look fine *now*!"

***

A few days after Wendy's wedding, Bernadette and I did get a marriage license, and were married at the clerk's office a week later, on a Monday. Bernadette wore stretchy jeans, because she was already starting to gain weight, and an embroidered tee-shirt, but she looked pretty. It didn't matter to me what she wore. When I came home, I found Gabriella sitting in front of the house with a Buick Regal she bought us as a wedding present, saying she was concerned about the beat-up Escort I drove, and that a bigger car would be safer for the baby. I was ecstatic, but Bernadette was annoyed by it because she felt it was another example of her mother meddling in her life.

We had no honeymoon of any kind, but I asked for a few days off from work so that Bernadette and I could get an apartment together and arrange to move in. We got lucky in finding an apartment we could afford in a newly converted warehouse. We had nearly the whole floor. She was working at a cosmetics counter then, which was ironic, because before she started there, I'd never seen her wear much more than brush on lip color— "lip stain," she called it.

The day after I went back to work, Gabriella called to ask me to come to their house without Bernadette to have a talk, to get to know each other.

Bruce and Gabriella's house was more than twice the size of Dad's. It was a three-story square, stucco building with tall, narrow windows on the first floor, an almost flat roof, and a little four-windowed room at the top that must have provided a wonderful view in a neighborhood lined with several other houses that were just as stately, and with similar manicured lawns.

Before I could ring the bell, Gabriella greeted me at the door.

"Come in, come in! I saw the car turn in. Do you like it?"

"Yes. I'm not used to driving a car that big. It's hard to maneuver, but I am getting used to it."

"I hate driving at all with the all the speed demons on the road," she said. "But it *is* a necessity."

The front door opened to a curved staircase and long hallway that led straight to French doors in the back. There were large archways that opened to a living room to the right, and a room with a grand piano and bookshelves on the left. Much of the trim was decorated in gold leaf.

"Thank you again. I wasn't expecting a car. That's very generous."

"It's not a *new* car, but it's in excellent condition," she said, putting her arm around my shoulder and giving me a brief squeeze. "So nice to spend time with you, Vincenzo. We can chitchat like mama and son now."

"You have such a beautiful house," I said.

"Thank you. It was in Bruce's family for three generations. To be honest with you, it was a bit of a dump when we moved in. No one had taken proper care of it. So, we made improvements over the years," she said, and then turned to face me. "I married a good man with a good family."

"How do you keep it up so nice? That must be a full-time job."

"We have a maid who comes in."

"I never met anyone with a maid."

Gabriella laughed. "It's not so special. Come sit down."

She led me into the room with the piano.

"Sit down," she said. "You drink coffee, I hope?"

"Sometimes," I said.

"Good! Not drinking coffee is a sin! I will bring some, fresh brewed."

"Do you need help?" I asked.

Gabriella smiled broadly and clasped her hands together. "You are such a sweet boy! Thank you, but I can get it," she said, pointing her finger.

After she had left the room, I stood and went over to look at the books.

"How do you take it?" Gabriella shouted from another room.

"Cream and sugar!" I shouted back.

"I do too!"

Many of the books on the far side of the room looked to be at least a hundred years old, with leather-bound covers. I didn't dare touch them. Most of the newer books, which were on the opposite wall behind the piano, were crime stories and murder mysteries—Agatha Christie, Raymond Chandler, Mickey Spillane, and so on, but also there were several history books on the World Wars, Korea, and Vietnam.

When Gabriella returned with the coffee, I asked, "Are you a fan of murder mysteries?"

"Oh no," she said putting the cups down on coasters on the table. "Those books are my husband's. The older books are mine, mostly to collect. I used to read occasionally, but I'd rather watch a good movie lately."

"I'm a reader," I said. "I like books more than movies, because I can make up the scenes and characters in my head just how I want them to look."

"I never thought of it that way! I suppose that is an advantage," she said, admiring her book collection. "Anyway, I take care of my husband now and so there is not so much time, but he is doing better than he was only a month ago. Steps by little steps."

"Where is he?"

"Upstairs, watching TV. I told him you were coming, but to let the two of us chat."

Gabriella sat on the other end of the sofa, then watched me, smiling with her hands folded in her lap.

She sipped her coffee, and then asked, "Are you in love with our daughter?"

"Yes, I am."

"I suppose it does not matter, as long as you are able to build a family."

"I do love her though. I wouldn't have married her if I didn't."

"That's not the only reason, or even the most important one, to be married."

"I think my mother married for material reasons. I imagine that's what it was from the story I was told. I don't want it to be like that. I want it to be true love that'll last forever."

Gabriella looked at me then, her mouth slightly open, like a butterfly collector discovering a new species. That's the best way I can describe it.

"She is difficult, you know. We did what we could with her, but my husband flew for the airlines and was away for days. So, it was only me most of the time."

"She seems like a good girl to me. She has some problems, but we all have problems."

Gabriella put the cup to her lips and her eyes seemed to glaze over. She took a long sip and set it back down onto the coaster.

"My husband and I wanted many children. We're Catholic. That is what we do; we have babies, but complications were discovered when I was carrying Bernadette. I almost died giving birth, and I could have no more."

"You could have adopted more," I said, feeling a bit sorry for her then. I felt we were connecting.

"Not the same thing." Gabriella smiled for a moment, but then looked sad, squinting at the floral pattern of her coffee cup for a moment. "Not to me."

Gabriella shook her head, sipped her coffee again, and then set it on the coaster—first the edge, then a semi-circular rotation, then down. She did everything with elegance, as if she were an actress in an old silver screen film.

"Bernadette told me about your family. I feel sorrow that your mother passed on when you were young," she said. "But you have your father, and you are close?"

"I was thirteen when she died. It was the worst thing that could have happened then."

"I can't imagine. My mother and brothers still live in Sicily, and I miss them every day. We visit when we can."

"I bet it's beautiful there."

"To me, no. There are many poor people back home, but it is important to see my family. Mama will not be with us for much longer."

She went quiet again, so I broke the silence with something she might be happy to hear.

"Mom, I'll be an excellent dad. Do you want me to call you 'Mom'? I wasn't sure."

"That would be wonderful."

"And after we have this one—and it's going to be a girl—we'll have more."

Gabriella smiled, but her eyes were downcast, so I continued. "I can handle all this. I know what I'm doing."

She motioned her hand toward the piano. "Do you play?"

"No. My mom played electronic keyboards when I was little, but I've never even been in the same room as a full-sized piano."

"It is a baby grand, so not near full-sized."

Gabriella went to the piano, sat on the bench, and then opened the cover to the keyboard.

"Listen!"

She motioned me to come, and when I stood up, she patted the bench next to her, and I sat down.

"Are you familiar with Glenn Gould?" she asked.

"I don't think so. Is he a singer?"

"Some say he is." She laughed a bit, but she still seemed less happy than when I first arrived. I couldn't put my finger on it. "That's a criticism of his vocalizations. But, no, only a pianist—my favorite—and you look a bit like him, as a young man, Vincenzo, except more handsome."

My face went hot.

She reached to her left and switched on a stereo.

"This is a recording of Gould playing Liszt."

She closed her eyes and swayed on the bench to the music. She did this for several minutes. I felt awkward, not knowing if I should interrupt her enjoyment.

"Who is your favorite composer?" I asked her when the piece ended. "An Italian probably, right?"

"Not so much Italian composers. Most have passion but lack much sense of beauty. I do like the classics: Bach, Mozart, but also some Debussy," she said, switching off the stereo.

"I know their names, but not anything they wrote. I don't listen to classical music. No offense, but it's kind of boring to me. I listen to heavy metal in the car."

"That's a shame, but you should try listening to a few Debussy pieces. It is soothing music, contemplative. It might help your thinking."

"I will try that," I said. "So, I guess you play the piano."

"Yes." She seemed to perk up a bit. "Let me teach you some songs that our family knows by heart."

"Great. I'd love to hear you play it."

"This is a common Sicilian folk song, one that everyone knows. Bernadette knows it very well."

She began to plunk the piano keys with her index fingers, as if she were searching for the letters on a typewriter, one at a time, then she sang, a little off pitch, in a quavering voice.

> *"Ciuri, Ciuri, Ciuri di tuttu l'annu*
> *l'amuri ca mi dasti ti lu tornu.*
> *Ciuri, Ciuri, Ciuri di tuttu l'annu*
> *l'amuri ca mi dasti ti lu tornu.*
> *La-la-la-la-la-la-la-la-la-la-la.*

"That was a song we sang in Sicily, but the words are in Corsican." She scowled. "That is only the first verse. It means:

"Flowers, flowers, flowers all the year

The love you gave *me*, I give you back!

"A nice song. Here is another," she said, and resumed pecking out keys.

> *E la luna 'n 'menzu o' mari*
> *mamma mia m'ha' maritari*
> *figghia mia a 'ccu t'ha a dari*
> *mamma mia pensici tu.*
>
> *Si ti dugnu a lu chiancheri*
> *iddu va iddu veni*
> *la sasizza 'n manu teni*
> *si ci pigghia la fantasia*
> *ti sasizzìa figghiuzza mia.*
> *E la luna 'n 'menzu o' mari*

She then breathed deeply, as if exhausted, and tucked a loose strand of hair behind her ear.

"I probably shouldn't sing that. It's a bit dirty, but funny. That verse is about a butcher and his sausage," she said with a bit of a chuckle, then put her arm around my shoulders and gave me another quick squeeze.

Gabriella then suddenly sat up straight and tapping her fingers of one hand on the palm of the other, she said, "Do you know, Vincenzo, when you have trouble making a decision?"

"Yes," I said, "but it's more like I make bad ones."

"I know. I see it." She waved her hand, dismissing a thought, then stood up from the bench. "There was something I did when I was a little girl." She pulled a book from the bookcase next to the piano, and then continued. "I used to do this when I had a difficult time putting my thoughts together. I still do sometimes if I am confused."

"I can't imagine you get confused."

"It happens now and then, but when *you* do, choose any book. Don't think much about which book, and then ask your question. Open the book to the right page for you, poke your finger at a line, and there is your answer!"

"How do I know it's the right place?" I asked.

"You trust your intuition."

Gabriella then closed her eyes. "Will my first grandson be healthy and happy?"

She opened the book and put her finger down on a spot on a page, then opened her eyes and read the line aloud.

"Something happened which aroused your suspicions?" suggested Poirot.

"It is like that," she said, closing it.

"Did that answer the question?" I asked.

"In a way, it answered it," she said and shrugged.

VIII. Pandora

On the way to moving back home in June, I saw that someone spray-painted in silver on the red brick wall outside of the abandoned factory building about halfway between Alex's place and the house. It wasn't there the last time I drove those blocks. Whatever it was, it was illegible—letters, or numbers, maybe just symbols surrounded by stars and circles. I slowed down to look at it and then noticed a man sitting below the graffiti with a cloth sack over this head like a hood. I think it was part of a burlap bag, the kind of bags that they sell animal feed in. I didn't notice him at first, because he was sitting among some empty cardboard boxes, scrap wood, tires, or whatever other trash was discarded there over time, and he blended into those things with his worn, grey clothes like a kind of camouflage.

I stopped the car. I'd stuffed my things without much thought into boxes and bags, and then stacked those on the seats and trunk. If he needed to go somewhere, I couldn't help with that.

Move on! Move on!

The thing's words echoed in my head. I understood them, and so I hesitated for a minute to roll down the window. Instead, I looked over to the passenger seat, and then I gripped the steering wheel hard. A green pickup truck, rusted and dented, came from the opposite direction and pulled over.

"Oh, great," I said under my breath.

The driver was a man with a red bushy beard, wearing a white tee-shirt. He leaned over to the passenger side and yelled over.

"You need any help?"

Of course I needed help, but I didn't know what kind I needed.

"I'm checking on this man to see if he's okay."

The man in the pickup looked around and over my car, squinting, then shook his head and waved himself off with a stiff hand.

The homeless man didn't seem to notice the truck nor that I stopped near him. If he did, he didn't look over at me. I decided to roll the window down.

"Hey!" I shouted. "You all right?"

He said nothing and didn't move. Maybe he was sick. Maybe he had died out here by the street. Some people have died sitting up. I've read that.

"Hey!" I shouted again.

Again, he didn't move. I waited.

"Hey!"

I opened the door. I heard murmuring or low humming, like a whisper. In the calm air, the whooshing of it tickled my ear. I stood just outside the driver's door and then shut it—slammed it.

"Hey!"

It was warm, humid. Clouds shrouded the sky in a thick, grey blanket that muted colors. It should have been cooler. I took a step in the man's direction.

"Hey, buddy."

I heard the murmuring more clearly. I realized then that it was the man. He was mumbling, muffled, though not to me. He hadn't acknowledged me. I walked in a semicircle to face him.

"Hey, you okay?" I took a deep breath.

I inched to within a few feet of him. He smelled of sour milk and cat piss. I think it was coming off him or at least from his direction. I decided I wouldn't have allowed him in the car anyway. I didn't dare get closer. The cloth sack covered the upper half of his face and nose, though he had a strip cut open across his eyes to see. What I could see myself of his face was covered with a silver and black beard. What I saw of his skin was dark and greasy, like the filth was embedded into it.

"Hey." Deep breath. Deep breath.

He was crouched down and bent forward, as if sitting by a campfire that wasn't there—squatting, maybe. I hadn't noticed if there were anything under him. He stared at something ahead and down, near a plastic cup in the dirt just to my right. He continued talking in the whisper, a monotone like a witchdoctor focusing on casting a spell.

"Hey," I said once again. "Do you need help, maybe a doctor?"

I looked around then, realizing that, for probably the first time, I had lost track of the thing.

"I can call an ambulance."

I backed away as I spoke. I felt I should just get back inside the car and leave.

Before I could take more than a few steps away, he sprang up from his spot near the ground. I set off to run back to the car, but he planted himself in front of me in the litter, like a cricket or a frog ready to spring again. Then he reached out to me. I threw up my hands to protect my face, preparing myself for an attack. Instead, he grasped my wrists and held them together, like they were in handcuffs.

"It didn't go away!" he shouted hoarsely, followed by deep coughing that sent a glob of spittle onto my shirt.

I wrenched my hands free and ran for the car. I didn't dare turn to see if he were following, but the street was quiet enough that I was sure I would have heard his footfalls.

Sitting down and closing the car door, I closed my eyes. I wished I could drive blind, just guided by my other senses. I didn't want to open them.

When I did open my eyes again, I kept my eyes fixed forward on the street ahead, which continues, almost uninterrupted, to the house, and that was good, because I'd forgotten for a moment how the car worked while driving it. I had to deliberately think about where the brake and accelerator were or how to signal. The sky grew darker as I approached the old block.

I turned into the driveway, and I was back at The White Elephant again, to not leave again for a long time. Thanks to Dad's living trust, the family house went into my hands without the months of probate. I was thankful for that because, in spite of what happened, I'd convinced myself that anything would be better than Alex's apartment, but I didn't consider all the pain that would come flooding back within seconds, and it hurt, even before I unpacked a box. I was sure the painful feeling would be there, but I didn't realize how much I hadn't forgotten.

I approached the back steps with the keys in my hand, when a heavy, egg-shaped, black shadow eclipsed my path ahead. It filled me with nauseating dread coming up from my guts. The thing, appearing again, close to the ground at my ankles, chased it away as quickly as it appeared, leaving behind a thread of silvery smoke. I learned that it would always be there to protect me; it would, at least until being there for me counted the most.

I stood outside the door for a full five minutes to collect my feelings, taking a few deep breaths—in through my nose and out through my mouth, like on *Lilias, Yoga and You* always said on PBS. She was so beautiful with her long braid.

It wasn't the same house now that I owned it. It was no better or worse, but like the thing, it belonged to me now. It wasn't "home," like I would tell other kids when I was a boy at school, "I'm going straight home after this," but that it was now a real building of wood and brick that I was responsible for, rather than a picture in my head to dream about, and I could only guess at what was inside.

I was wrong again. While I turned the key in the lock, I realized that *I* belonged to the *house*—that *it* owned *me*. It didn't let me go but waited until Dad was gone to reach out its arms and pull me back in, and when I built up the nerve to walk in, I saw that it *did* change. I went directly through and out of the kitchen, as if it were never there. I needed to see the living room. I first looked up at the ceiling. I'm not sure why, but I was sad to see that it had false beams now in some kind of wood stained a dark brown. Had Dad done this himself alone? It looked like quite a job to finish without help.

Move on! Weitergehen!

No. I could see that it wasn't the same house I left, though I'd last seen the inside of it not even a full three years ago. It smelled different, animalic, like the musky smell of those bucks hanging from their antlers at the hunting camp, but also something sickly sweet like overripe bananas; and the mirrors, the small, round one with the silver frame in the living room, and the bigger, square one in the dining room were gone. They had been there since Mom and I moved in.

The stairs were wrong. What was it? The banister was red—just the handrail. No. It was grey last I saw it. Was it? Yes. Nothing had primary colors here after Mom died. Dad couldn't stand bright colors. He said they looked childish, like a kindergarten. Chrome, white, black marble, the brown of the woodwork, those were what he could settle into—anything industrial, metallic. I sniffed the paint. It still smelled like latex. It was a bad job. Some of the red had dripped down, and there were a few spots on the steps. Dad would have never let that happen. All the pictures—those that had people in them—were also gone, put away somewhere, except one.

I looked toward the table—or console, whatever—under the window.

Get out! This is my father's house!

"Dad, why? Why did you hide the rest of the pictures, but leave one of you and Daisy? It must have been from when you first brought her home from the shelter. Right there for me to see. Did you know? Who took it?"

It was worse than the messy paint job, the smell of rotting fruit, and the close dampness. It wasn't like the home I left. It was much worse.

"Dad? You said you loved me, so why would you be so cruel to leave me this—or that, if I'm not really here—blinding, white house? I agreed, but what choice did I have then? And I didn't expect you to die—not for a long time, and when you did, I hoped things would be right again, and maybe better. Now, I'm forced to face the sun shrieking in through the venetian blinds like a nightmare at the back again, and all the darkness and creeping monsters ready to pounce on me from the corners where the light doesn't reach.

"I've felt before like I wasn't where I thought I was. I'm having that feeling again. Maybe, this is another dream. Maybe I fell asleep after I parked the car and I'm not really here, but there's the thing in the corner under the stairs with its glowing eyes. That's there! Maybe this is a game playing in my imagination. Maybe I was taken away and it followed me, but you left it to me to move back to—I know that much. You did die—to remind me of the blood, the horrors, the things that I had to clean. Those are the things I don't need to remember. Those are the things I spent nearly three years forgetting. I became good at forgetting."

I started up the stairs to the bedrooms, bathroom, and your office. I don't know what work you did there. I only saw you watching the TV the few times the door was open. First it was the room you and Mom set aside in case she got pregnant and we needed another bedroom, but she never did—and never wanted to, and so, bit by bit, you moved your own stuff in there. You didn't even allow me in there. Remember? Now it's mine.

Du musst dich ausruhen!

The thing is whispering German now! It knows I understand *sehr wenig* German. Very little. Spanish, yes. French, some. German, no. It's teasing me. Try to remember!

When I opened the door and walked in the office—that room—not for the first time in years, but the first time since we first moved in with Mom, I needed to explore why it was off limits. I didn't find anything interesting though, not right away, just a desk and chair, your nursing textbooks on a narrow shelf, the leather recliner—that was what happened to it—an old-fashioned dart board behind shutters, the TV in an entertainment center.

Nothing was in the top drawer of the desk but a handful of pens, a notebook—a few pages filled with some chicken scratches and tally marks counting something—I don't know—utility bills, receipts for hardware items. Two drawers were empty, except for fluffs of dust, and the smell of candle wax and something sharp, like gunpowder. In the bottom drawer, I found the financing paperwork for the car and educational loans, torn open envelopes of mail about insurance or credit offers. There were also my court papers from when you adopted me. They were also there.

I played Frank Hardy a little more by looking into the closet, where you had winter coats hanging and your hunting boots on the floor, near the rifle. When was the last time you hunted? But there is a shelf over the clothing rod. That was empty too, I thought, but I couldn't know for sure until I brought your chair over, because I couldn't see, or feel far on that shelf with my hands.

"When I stepped up, I found the box. You picked a pretty one, red foil with a silver stripe up each side to look like ribbons, the kind of box they use to gift-wrap at the stores. I opened it up to find rings, bracelets, gold chains, a few earrings on a plastic tree, and some on those little plastic cards. On top of them was the scrawled note. Your handwriting was crap, even if you were careful, but it must have been a last-minute decision, because you didn't even bother to find a clean sheet of paper, which would have been about ten feet away. You knew what you were doing, and I did what you wanted, and I'll quote it.

Here Son,

This is your Mom's jewelry. You hated (I'll guess that's what that word was) it, so give it to Bernie.

Dad

"I know why you did it! I know why! I know why! But why was it written on the back of a receipt from Pep Boys, dated the day before your accident? Mom died thirteen years ago! I hate when you think I'm stupid, like when you thought I didn't know how to fire the rifle, when I was only afraid to do it! The people I meet every day think I'm a stupid boy—just a boy! Worst of all, the thing believes I'm stupid! It doesn't respond to me! Oh, my god, Dad!

Mom! It doesn't even talk to me like I'm a grown human! Then it broke its promise, or maybe I broke mine. How will I ever tell a girl I love her? I'll need to tell someone someday just that very thing!"

IX. How Terrible Is Wisdom

Mom's mom and dad were florists, and so she learned that red carnations are for yearning hearts, white roses for innocence, and violets for modesty. They owned a shop on a corner downtown. It's closed now. I don't know why it closed, but Grandpa Thelin bought it just after they married. Grandpa knew nothing of the business, but bought it for Grandma, who was wise in the language of the flowers. She knew how they were arranged for any occasion, and together they made happy bouquets to cheer the ill, to express first love, to celebrate a marriage, to bring home a new baby, and to honor the dead. There were certain flowers for certain occasions: Roses for weddings, chrysanthemums for funerals. The traditional choices were best because they would offend no one.

When Mom was a girl with copper penny hair, she would sometimes spend Saturdays in the shop while they accepted deliveries and filled special orders. Hyacinths and white lilies would come in the spring, when the sprouting bulbs were trucked in from the supplier. Hyacinths smell like cotton candy. In the fall, poinsettias arrived by the dozens. In the winter, more potted houseplants came in. The showers of mist from overhead sprayers made the caretaking place in the store a magical English garden. Hidden from the street by a wall of red brick and glass blocks, she would peer out behind the floor arrangements like a sprite exploring secret orchards.

That was Mom of her girlhood flower shop stories, the stories that painted a picture in my head, but seemed nothing like the mom I knew as a grown woman. She mentioned that she had an older brother who was already in middle school when she was born, but she said they weren't close. I never met him, and he never came around. She laughed, telling me how she called broccoli "flower trees," and that she liked them with apple cider vinegar. I don't remember her ever cooking broccoli, though I liked it too. She loved pickles and would eat them off other people's hamburgers when we went out to get fast food, but she grew odder as the years passed, at least the way I saw it. Maybe we all are when we get older, and that's why most of us get batty as clock towers by the time we're ninety and living in a nursing home.

After everything that's happened, and though I was still a boy, thirteen years doesn't seem like an awfully long time ago. It wasn't too hot or too cold then, at least I don't remember becoming dizzy from the sun pressing down on my head like it does now, or that my neck and shoulders turned red and burned as quickly as they do. Plans worked just the way they should have when I think back on it. There was no pain, and if there was, it was followed by simple pain or fever relief, or an appointment with the friendly doctor, who was always quick to write a prescription.

Just after I turned nine, during one of dad's Thanksgiving hunting trips with me, my feet got wet. Mom was always afraid I'd get hurt, and I didn't like to go hunting anyway. I had to get out of bed in time to leave before the sun was up and then walk around in the cold where there were bears. We never bagged an animal, ever—not even a rabbit if they were in season—but we'd always have to drive out to some guy's metal garage afterward where other hunters were hanging their deer by their antlers for a few days to age the meat.

I didn't understand why deer season had to happen in freezing weather after a layer of snow was usually on the ground and with soft leaves under the slush. Dad used some jargon about the "thick of rut," which meant nothing to me, and I don't know why it did to him. He just wasn't the kind of guy I could ever imagine hunting. He was thin, wore glasses, and had a receding hairline—not an image of the great warrior.

"What's the matter, son?"

I was stopped dead on the spot, shivering. My teeth were chattering.

"I can't feel my feet."

"They hurt? Like glass?"

I nodded. "Before, yeah. They felt crunchy. Now I can't feel them."

"Did you get water in your boots?" He rested his rifle against a tree and squeezed the toes of my boots. "Dammit, son."

He hugged me.

"There was a puddle back there." I pointed behind me. "Deeper than a puddle. I thought it was frozen over, but no. I went right in. Quoosh."

"Aw, I'm sorry, little man."

He hugged me a long time, until I warmed up.

"We need to get you home. Keep the boots on for now."

When I got home, I took my boots off myself. I screamed as I did it. My feet were swollen, whitish, and blotchy. I couldn't move my left foot without extreme pain, and I still had no feeling in the right one, even after I was thawed out. Mom took me to see the pediatrician, Dr. Zimmerman, when my toes started to bleed.

"Soak his feet in warm water with soap suds, then keep them dry. They will feel better," the doctor said to Mom and then pinched and patted my cheek. "And don't wear socks to bed!"

More than once when I was a boy, the rare trips out of town with The Who's "Baba O'Reilly" roaring out of the car stereo, were for Mom, where she'd get a prescription or an injection, but at least a helpful suggestion with a smile, like it was simply good customer service. In that way, medicine is like any other quality service. One time it was clear that something happened out of the ordinary.

"You need to watch yourself, Mrs. Pelletier," Dr. Dutta said to her in his musical Indian accent, and then wrote her a prescription. "Take the pill, one dose," he said, and then he looked to me sitting on the stool. He reached behind himself to a cabinet and pulled out a sugar-free sucker, then handed it to me.

Dr. Dutta patted me on the cheek and said, "There you go! How's that!"

"Thank you," I said, while unwrapping it to put in in my mouth. It was cherry, I think.

"Don't like to say too much with the boy around," said Dr. Dutta that day, smiling in a way that looked strained.

"I can't leave him home," Mom said. "My husband works during the day."

"There are clinics closer to home for you."

"In town. I know."

"Okay, so you need to stay at your home more, with family and not doing other things, so you are not taking unnecessary trips. You know what I am saying?"

Mom looked as if she would spit at him. "You're supposed to be a doctor, not my daddy."

"I am only saying that—"

"I don't need a daddy. I can take care of my own business. You just take care of my health!"

Not much worth mentioning changed between that strange visit with Dr. Dutta, or when I was riding my yellow bike with clattering metal beads Mom put on the spokes, and the day I went to college, except that she died. Nothing happened that I want to mention now.

I applied at the college not so much for a good job or better pay, but because it would help me find my own brain, and I also wanted to have a reason to end all the calls from the military recruiters. But instead of any self-awareness, I simply got older.

Whoever lived three houses to the right finally had a dead tree removed. I grew a few more inches—not much; I wasn't tall. Love, maybe. Yes, that changed, the who and the how—but I can't even think about that, or who I would call "my baby" on one day or the next. Love was complicated, and I was alone.

By the last year or so before Mom died, she'd spend too much time on the couch—at least according to Dad—staying up late, watching the late-night talk shows in her fuzzy slippers and wrapped in a blanket. She was almost always cold in the house, no matter how hot Dad felt or how high she set the thermostat. She once wore earmuffs in the house when it was particularly cold outside, but sometimes the very next day, she'd feel hotter than Dad did, and she'd say she had to take a cool shower. Her feet and head were continually nodding back and forth to some disco beat that was in her head, sometimes with humming.

She loved her big, dangling earrings and spent forever in the morning on her eyebrows with tweezers or putting on eyeliner with her shaky hands. She wore jewelry that made noise—necklaces that jingled like bells and bangle bracelets that clanked together. I always knew she was nearby when we were out shopping. I didn't like the sound of the jewelry because I wanted quiet. Mom was never quiet.

Dad's work hours changed from day to day. I didn't know when he would be home or out, but when he wasn't home, *Mom* would be out. She never left me alone for long, even by the time I was old enough. It was as if she didn't trust me, but she would leave me inside while she went out to talk to one or another guy in a car I didn't know. When Dad worked nights, she'd even let this one guy with a bad cough in the house, but it was rare that anyone came in. She thought I was asleep, I think, but I sleep light, and noises would wake me up, no matter how quiet they tried to be.

I wanted to know where the blood came from in the bathroom wastebasket, but until I was about nine or ten, I was afraid to ask. It stayed confined to the bathroom, the place where our most secret and intimate activities hide, and so first I thought it might be none of my business. The blood was absorbed into what I called "tissue pillows," but by the time I was in fifth grade, I started to play detective, and discovered that the blood in the bathroom coincided with the days that Mom would put Xs on the kitchen calendar that hung from the pantry door. I imagined myself Encyclopedia Brown, but it was a puzzle, and so I came out and asked. That's what Mom would do if she were me.

"Mom, what's the blood in the bathroom?"

"Who was bleeding in the bathroom? Nate probably cut himself again," she said.

"I think it was you. I'm talking about the blood in the wastebasket."

She cackled in one rowdy burst.

"Oh, yes, me. Don't worry about that," she said and then rolled her eyes. "You'll learn all that later on."

After that talk, she wrapped the things up in multiple layers, and we never had that other talk. I learned about it on my own when I was older, but she never wanted to explain anything to me. She was either busy or too absorbed in the TV or her music. I learned all about women on my own, and I didn't think it was a big deal. I would have been relieved to know when I first asked. About a year after that, she had her "tubes tied," as she called it, but it wasn't a big deal to know about that either.

***

They buried Mom outside of town. I'm not sure where. If I had to get to the cemetery myself, I don't think I'd know the way. I never visited her grave after the interment, but Dad did often. He never asked me to go because he thought it would be traumatic for me. So, he'd go up there if I were in school. I remember her grave was just through the gate and to the right, and that there's an angel on her headstone, but as for the cemetery, I know it's out in the countryside and that she was buried next to her older sister, who died as a child in an accident when she was thrown from the car. If she lived to be about ten or eleven, and Mom died when she was 37, then was she still older? It's strange how that works.

I didn't want to visit there anyhow, because it didn't make sense to talk to the grass or a gravestone. That wasn't where she was. If I wanted to talk to Mom, it would be to the photo of her on the wall in the living room at the bottom of the stairs. We were coloring Easter eggs. Dad caught me at a happy moment, laughing, as she looked on. I talked to that picture almost every day after school. There was no confusion then. Yes, lots of whispering on the far side of the boxwoods, yet only more questions to answer.

X. "Who's he when he's at home?"

Being outside at night with dusk, and then darkness closing in on me, especially with the glaring floodlights overhead, feels something like a dream, maybe because my parents never let me go out alone in the dark. I don't mean it was *surreal*, but anytime I've gone into the night—not downtown where there was nightlife and noise, but when I was alone, and the air was still—I questioned whether I was only imagining each image I saw around me. Nighttime walks alone were always that way, especially in the spring when the temperature hovered in the space between warm and cold, and that peculiar funereal smell was in the air, like wildflowers and damp earth. It's chilling on the skin, yet tiny beads of sweat still formed on my face.

When walking the warehouse yard at work, the utility lights blocked out the stars, and I was caged in a vacuum of time and space. Sometimes, it was hard to see the moon, even when it was full. Looking up, there were the blinding lights, and, above that, a damp, black flannel covering the sky, and so quiet that I was sure I could hear my heartbeat, if it weren't for the unending electrical buzz.

We weren't armed at the warehouse, and we weren't allowed to bring a gun onto the site if we had one. They didn't even give us a club, just a phone to call the police. I never had to do it, and I can't imagine a criminal breaking in because we were so far from real life. The police would probably take a long time to show up if anyone *did* break in. The only valid reason for having a guard was to discourage thieves from coming over the fence if they were determined enough to do it. If one did, he could just shoot at me if he wanted, and I couldn't do anything about it, but the company believed that a live human walking the yard would be a deterrent, while the security cameras and barbed wire were not. A thief wouldn't care about the cameras if they wanted to break in bad enough, and they could disguise themselves with a mask if they *did* care. The fence wasn't difficult to climb, as my boss demonstrated himself during my training, in case I doubted it.

I was having trouble staying awake the morning I first saw the thing and it came into me. There were a few mornings that I had trouble keeping my eyes open, but I'd never fallen asleep at work. I forced myself to stay on my feet so that I never would. The girl who worked my nights off was there a year longer than me, so she wasn't worried about following the training manual, and she was less vigilant. She'd spend half her time in the booth, listening to the radio or talking to her girlfriend on the phone, but I nearly dozed off the first night I worked alone. I didn't want to lose an easy job that paid well, so I stayed out of there unless it was to make coffee or eat my lunch, and most of the time, I stood while I did those things.

I didn't work my full shift that night because they had an inventory scheduled. The executives came in without warning with the crew. The car and the vans' headlights, and the crunch of their wheels on the gravel jolted me back to attention. The suits and inventory people spoke little to me, aside from "hey" and "how's it going?" A few minutes later, my boss called and said that I could go home if I liked. I could stay for the rest of the shift if I wanted, but I hadn't slept much the day before, because Alex would not turn down—what was that music he was listening to?—Faith No More? I was sharing an apartment with him at the time, after Bernadette and I were divorced. He was a student for many years and would probably never graduate. His grandmother sent him money whenever expenses got out of hand, so he wasn't going anywhere anytime soon and he's probably still living there.

The security guards parked inside the fence, and we had to pull open the gate by hand to get in and out. The gate was heavy and rolled on wheels. I had to almost move the weight of one car to drive another home, but I had gotten used to doing this after a week or two on the job, and I didn't even think about it. The girl could do it herself, so I couldn't complain. Still, the gate felt heavier than usual that morning, as if it were lead instead of steel. The air felt heavier too, and still—dew settled on the surfaces, and the droplets glistened in the lights.

I left the warehouse just before 4 a.m., taking the usual route home, which had nothing along it other than a John Deere dealership about a mile down. After that, there were stretches of bony trees broken by patches of open, grassy fields. Occasional animals in the grass and branches looked out, their eyes reflecting the headlights. Just past the city limit sign was a group of dilapidated houses with broken windows—I'm sure people didn't live in them—and an abandoned garage. Half a mile toward home was a cemetery, and next, the large woodlot, which was a block on the back side of one of the better neighborhoods, and a few blocks from Alex's place.

Although it was about thirty feet from the road, the thing was easy to spot because it had a glow that was brighter around its eyes and jaws—almost reddish. It was peculiar enough to bring me to pull the car over and get out to see what it was.

The thing was a haze at first at the edge of the deeper woods, like steam rising from an open manhole on a cold night, but denser and well-shaped, like I could put my arms around it, and for a moment I wished I could. It rose to about the level of the wrought iron fence a few yards ahead and then it began to drift—drifting toward me. It was 4 a.m., and I had just gotten out of work. No other car had been on the road for ten or fifteen minutes, but the thing was there.

I wasn't sleeping or sleepwalking. Some people can do that, even when they drive, and I have dreams, at times, that I've told myself were hallucinations, but I had just left the worksite. My boss had talked to me. I had met with workers. I had pushed open the big gate. All of that was more real than anything at the time. I could still feel the cold of the metal gate handle on my palms. I had driven the car for over two miles, and I was awake. I was careful to stay alert. I'd been in accidents before that weren't my fault.

After I got out of the car, the form moved fully into the thin, young trees that were nearest the road, and just sprouting new leaves, but after I took a few steps into the brush, my boot had sunk into a seep hidden under the tall grasses that left a thick layer of mud in the deep treads of the sole. I stepped up and onto a flat spot of ground, covered with a bit of loose gravel, but every step after was like walking through quicksand, my boot adhering to the ground.

On the far side of the woodlot, facing the other side the block, was one of the old Tudor Revival houses that were built at the turn of the century. I could just see the back yard, and with the setting moonlight, I saw the angels carved in marble, and concrete urns holding the annual plantings of mid-May petunias through the wrought iron fence. I saw each hedge and trellis in detail, as it should have been, even in the distant darkness. That entire setting was there. It was here. That thing was more real than me. It couldn't have been any trick of the shadows between the trees because the light from the streetlights streamed in between what trees there were.

It crept toward me by inches, and then it stopped, lowering its head, resting in one place, as if it were waiting for me to come closer, to greet it with a closed hand, but I couldn't move. My feet were rooted like the sycamores, and like them, I could only reach out. The thing remained still for a minute, before rising and moving sideways, in one direction, then the other, as if it were examining me. It did this for another minute before it stopped again, and then, like a fast-forwarding video, it rushed toward me, causing me to lose my breath.

It leaped up then, as if to jump into my arms, but instead, it went further, taking over and engulfing me, not in cold as I was certain it would, but in warmth—a soft, moist warmth—and at that second, I became a formless entity also. From that point—and more and more with time onward— it shared its thoughts with my thoughts, we breathed the same air, tasted the same scents on it, and we heard the same sounds in the same way from the same ears.

On the way home—Alex's home in reality and always—two turns and a minute further, I tried with my best ability to separate what I saw and heard from a daydream, but all the images were still dark. The sky was on a dimmer switch, coming on by degrees by the time I pulled up to the apartment building that morning, but the thing didn't disappear in the light. If there were a difference, the thing picked up the light, from inside and outside, and then reflected it back.

That morning at the apartment, in my cramped bedroom, cluttered with books and toys I saved from when I was a boy, it was no longer inside me. I could sense it moving out and away, but still near me. I felt strangely cold and alone, but in a minute, I saw it there, curled at the foot of my bed. Its eyes glowed in the darkness I made for myself each morning by pulling the black shades down. It stared into me, but remained silent.

I had trouble falling asleep with the new, strange presence. It's as if it were no longer my own bed. Even while doing nothing, it silently demanded my attention. It took me an hour or two to drift off, and when I did, I had a vivid dream. It was the kind I had when I had a fever as a boy, or I was sick with a bad winter cold.

My mom was alive, but we weren't at the house. We were in a ramshackle cabin, just through a gateway in a clearing that was in the middle of a kind of prehistoric forest of strange, skyscraping palm trees. She asked me to go out to collect firewood so she could cook our dinner.

"Bring us back some firewood, Vinny! Before it starts coming down!" she shouted too loudly, while she held a basket by the handle in the crook of her elbow.

I went out, and I saw we had a garden. It was just outside the door, with tomato plants and cabbages.

"Firewood for the stove!" she shouted out to me, sounding much farther away than she was. I was wearing a rough blanket of various stripes of color over my shoulders.

Gigantic, bat-winged birds screeched and circled in the sky, which was dark, and threatening rain. I heard something terrible, yet invisible, roar horribly in the distance, like an echoing explosion.

XI. The Wine-Pourer

Red Dot Lounge & Lanes was choked with thick, blue-grey cigarette smoke that left yellow stains on the walls, the ceiling fans, and the stalls in the restrooms. Three gum-chewing bowlers with "feathered back" hair and pink lipstick sat at the bar with their beer or pop after finishing a Saturday night of ladies' league games. No ordinance had yet banned smoking in bars, and there was quite a protest when one passed. The bar was at the front with the bowling alley in the back and, as was usual on the weekend, a cover band was playing. Roxanne Thelin, a green-eyed, freckled redhead, nearly six feet tall, was the vocalist, and she was accustomed to men like Nate Pelletier trying to pick her up while on a break. That much was nothing new to her.

Roxanne was behind the building, bouncing on her toes to keep herself warm and sneaking a joint with the drummer when Nate crept up behind her.

"Boo," he said and followed that with a high-pitched hoot.

Roxanne leaped a few inches from the ground and threw the joint into the tangled brush behind the chain-link fence.

"Jesus fucking Christ!" she said.

"Aw, I'm sorry," he said.

The drummer spat onto the concrete. "There was nothing left on it anyway."

"No, no," Nate said. "I'm sorry I scared ya."

Roxanne, who was a couple of inches taller than Nate, looked him up and down and sneered, "You're lucky, buddy, I didn't spin around and clock you."

"I'm sure you could, ma'am," Nate said, rubbing his nose and grinning.

The drummer looked at his watch and then to Roxanne. "We have to get back in ten. Wanna grab a drink first?"

Roxanne gave him a dismissive wave. "I'll be in in a few. I'll be fine."

"You sure?" asked the drummer, glaring suspiciously back and forth between Roxanne and Nate.

Nate shrugged, throwing his hands up. "I'm not a pervert."

Roxanne kept her eyes on Nate. "What are you doing back here anyway?" she asked, as the drummer disappeared through the back door.

"I had to pee—bad—and there was a line at the men's room, so I peed in the bushes over there, and then I saw you smoking."

"So, you had nothing to do after that, except scare the shit out of me."

"Well, I wanted to talk to ya anyway. You are a damned fine singer."

"Thanks," said Roxanne flatly, then folded her arms.

"Yeah, you could be doin' better than singing in a bowling alley."

"This is all I can do for now. Gigs are hard to get for a full band, and we all have day jobs that take up time."

"Well, I'm a paramedic myself. That takes up a *lot* of time with long hours. I know what you mean."

"No shit? I had you pegged for a mechanic or something," said Roxanne, raising her eyebrows.

"No, ma'am, I saved a life once or twice, probably."

"Speaking of that day job, I have the night job to finish, so I can get paid and go. I have a little boy at home, so it's a full day tomorrow."

"Honest to Pete? You're too young to have a kid. Bet he's cute as hell."

"He's the cutest kid I've ever seen, but he's all over the place, and being a mom scares the men away."

"So that means you have no husband or boyfriend?"

Roxanne took a moment to consider the consequences of her answer.

"No. It's just me."

"Well, damn, that don't scare me. I love little boys. I was one myself," he said with his chuckle. "I'm Nate, by the way," he said, offering his hand, palm up.

Roxanne looked confused, but then slid her palm across his. "Roxanne. I gotta get going back," she said, indicating the open rear door with her thumb.

"Do you do anything more than sing?" Nate said with a grin.

"If that's a proposition, then the answer is 'none of your business.'"

"No, no," he said, covering his face with his hand, then continued excitedly, "I mean can you play too? Guitar, bass, you know?"

"I play a little guitar, but I'm not great. Some keys. I'm pretty good at that."

"Well, damn, you sure are a great singer. You should be recording albums."

"Thanks again. Listen, I need to get back. We have one more set and we're out of here."

"All right, all right, can I talk to ya when you're finished?"

"I know you're trying to open a gateway, but... cool beans. I'll need to keep it short though. Kid, remember? I got the babysitter waiting."

"Well, that would be just dandy, Roxie."

"Roxanne. Never Roxie."

While the band finished their last set, Nate sat himself down at the bar, speaking to no one, but grinning in her direction and nodding his head to the music, drinking Coke so that he could drive home. When the band was finished, and said their goodnights, he watched Roxanne load the mic stand and amp into the van on the far side of the parking lot, and then waited while she smiled and chatted with the drummer who she waved off, before she reentered the bar.

"You do that song 'I Fall to Pieces' the best. That's country though, right?"

"We do anything from the fifties or sixties, pop and rock mostly, but we throw in some country, and that song's one of my favorite singles."

"Yeah, yeah, who sings that?" Nate snapped his fingers.

"Patsy Cline."

"Yeah, yeah, and that's who you sound like. Just like her."

"Thanks, in a big way, but we're *all* good." Roxanne looked over her shoulder and pointed to the guitarist still packing away his equipment. "Keith was a session player for Carole King."

"Well, that sure is somethin'."

"You talk kind of funny, Nate."

"You're probably catching my accent. I don't think I have one anymore. Most people don't hear it."

"At first, I thought you were a southern boy, but *no*... It's the Rs that got me. They sound Frenchy."

"Good guess. I'm from Quebec, a small town outside Montreal. My family spoke French at home."

"How'd you end up here?"

"Long story for another time, but I sure don't want to have to go back."

"And you're a paramedic, or something?"

"Yeah, yeah, I make good money. I bought a three-bedroom house for a steal last month on the other side of town. It's just needing some care and work on it. Made a down payment and got a mortgage anyway, but it's mine."

"Yeah? I have a little apartment downtown over my parent's store. But, hey, I need to call the sitter and let her know I'll be a little late. I'll be right back."

When she returned, Nate handed her one of the peonies that someone had left in a cut-glass vase on the other end of the bar.

"Well, look at you; you're a charmer," she said.

"Poor thing would have been wilted and dead by tomorrow. It's better to put it to good use," he said with a firm nod and a smile.

"Peonies are special flowers, you know. They pop up from the ground spring after spring for a hundred years and sometimes longer. They stand for..." Roxanne rolled her eyes up, searching the files of her memory. "Oh, compassion... and *bashfulness*."

"I picked a good one then."

"They all mean something. I'm not sure how much they apply."

"It's pretty and red and pink, like you. I know *that*."

"*You* look kind of like a weasel," Roxanne said with a smile. "But not in a bad way. Weasels are cutie pies."

"Why thanks, then!"

"And you have that little gap between your front teeth." She laughed.

"Why's that funny?"

"A friend in high school used to say something about men with a gap in the front."

Dates out for ice cream or milkshakes became regular, and then rides into the countryside outside of town with me in the back seat, asking Dad what Canada was like, though he'd never say more than "frigid, little boy, frigid" and then he'd change the subject. I called him "Dad" on our third outing. I was happy that he didn't seem to mind it. In turn, he called Mom "Big Red."

They married, in a little civil ceremony, a few months after they met. Mom wore a blue dress and one of Mom's coworkers was a witness. Dad brought his ambulance partner. Soon after that he moved us into the little white house, and Mom quit working full time and quit singing completely. I don't remember what the old apartment looked like at all, but I can recall that continual scent of wet flowers.

So, we had dinner at regular times each night and every night after she was a mom-wife, and I was a man-son, at least for a while. I had a friend and a buddy in my Dad. Not an evil, storybook stepparent, but a real friend who didn't want to tell me what to do or where I couldn't go every minute of the day like Mom did, but none of that lasted for long. What he wanted, she didn't, more and more often. She kept me by her side more every year. Mom wanted to keep track of me, but so did Dad in a different way.

—Shh, don't tell your mom, but I got you some of that crackling, popping candy stuff in my car. Those things are fun! I love those fuckers!

—I don't want him putting that crap in his mouth. It has to damage your stomach lining. I can't imagine they're good for you.

—Hey, Vinny, we don't have ketchup at this table. Go grab it for us from that table over there.

—Get the waitress! Don't creep it from another table. Jesus. What's wrong with you?

—I'm gonna take you out on a road trip to Vegas with me for my training. We'll be two men on the road. Sound like fun?

—You're not takin' him goddam anywhere! You're not running my son off to God-knows-where. You know better than that, you asshole!

—Always remember, no matter what happens, your Dad loves you. You got the best one ever, and you're the best little boy.

Eight years after they married, Mom died, and it was good that I wasn't home, but instead, I was about two hours away at a summer program for "at risk" boys. Before they sent me there, Mom and Dad had an argument about it. Neither one of them wanted me to be gone for the whole summer, but Dad said the discipline along with the exercise and outdoors would be good, because I wouldn't go out unless it was for school, and the winter before, I began to refuse to go hunting with him, because it was too cold and too early in the morning.

"It's so damned far away," Mom said. "I'm worried about all the bad influences you'll get mixed up with." She was on the verge of tears when she read off the things I was required to bring, and the items I was forbidden to bring.

"Jesus, Mary, and Joseph! He's not allowed to take his goddam sock bear!" she screamed down to Dad.

"Fucking Christ, he's thirteen, Roxanne!" Dad shouted back up.

I didn't care that much about it, one way or the other, even about being away, because I'd at least be able to make friends with kids who didn't already know me from my school and I could try to make good first impressions all over again. The program was the first time I had ever been that far from Mom, but they didn't leave us enough free time to think about it. It was the first time anyone forced me to get up at a specific time while school was out, or to take a shower for no longer than two minutes. I started out failing most of their tests, sometimes on purpose, thinking they would send me back home early, but I wasn't good with most of the physical fitness challenges anyway, and they still kept me. There were no girls there to flirt with either, which didn't help matters, but it wasn't bad at all. I met boys like me without judgments, and we had a lot of fun.

The day before she died was the first cool day of June, which was strange, since it was also the day before summer. Back home, people were using the day to turn off their ACs, to open the windows for a while, and to let in the fresher air from the hills. It was a welcomed change for me, because I couldn't stand the heat even more than I couldn't stand the cold, and it was too hot here most of the summers, most of the time. We'd just come back from a hike in the forest to identify edible and poisonous plants when I got the news and the counsellor helped me pack up my clothes.

Dad said that that night, he and Mom both went to bed earlier than usual and were asleep by around 9 p.m. at the end of *The Fall Guy*, which I guess is irony. It was strange, because I hadn't seen them sleep in their bedroom together for about a year. Mom slept on the couch most nights, which was comfortable enough in any case. They "drifted off to sleep a few minutes into it," he said, because they were both working hard in the back yard that day clearing out the brush behind the shed. I'd never seen Mom do yardwork, because she got sunburned after about two minutes outside, but maybe it was because she was bored by having me away, and because I wasn't there to help myself.

Dad said that he woke up once at midnight and heard her breathing just fine. He said he then fell asleep until a sudden gust of wind came out of nowhere and knocked over the picture from their wedding on the dressing table, which woke them both up. They talked for a minute, and then Mom said that she had a headache. Dad said that he got up out of bed and got her an aspirin and a glass of water—something else I had never seen him do before—and then he finally fell back to sleep again around 2 a.m. Dad said that when he awoke again at 4 a.m., she was not responsive. He moved her to the floor and applied his best CPR skills, but she had a little froth around her mouth, and he realized when he checked her pulse a few times that it was just too late.

The coroner ruled it sudden cardiac arrest due to an undiagnosed heart condition. Not anything that would normally cause arrhythmias in her sleep, but there was nothing suspicious in it. Dad gave up his ambulance job soon after Mom died and he went back to college to be a registered nurse because there was a bigger demand for that, and he could make more money.

After a couple of weeks of getting sympathetic phone calls and what few visitors we had at the house, Dad spent the first two or three weeks rearranging furniture and buying new things for the house. He took me out with him to pick out cabinets and fixtures for the kitchen in black granite and chrome, instead of the country blue, ragdolls, and pumpkins that Mom liked. He also replaced a lot of the pictures and art on the walls. I asked him to keep the Easter egg picture in its usual spot for me, because it was my favorite.

"You can put it in your room if you want," he said.

"But she didn't come into my room much. I'll feel like she is out here with me, watching TV and singing with me."

He left it there, though he eventually took that down too, after I got married and moved out.

He wanted me to go out with him everywhere, even if it was only a few minutes or if I had schoolwork to do, and if it were a store or garage or anyplace with people, I had to go in with him. In mid-August, Dad and I went out to get new drawer pulls for the kitchen cabinets, and some Christmas lights and hooks before we'd have a little birthday party for him, just him and me, at the house, and a cake he had decorated at the Safeway. Though Christmas was over four months away, Dad thought getting them now would save time and money later. We never decorated much before, but he wanted to keep up with the neighbors' houses on both sides of us. They both had elaborate decorations and our house looked drab and dark between them.

"Not much flashy shit. It's gotta be classy," he said, after getting the lights he wanted and while looking at the hardware to secure them. "I don't want it to look like we're in a goddam competition, or like the elephant is all whored up!"

"We got lots of time. If you want to get more later, you can."

"Sure, sure. We can."

"It'll look pretty though," I said.

Dad put his face up close to mine and said, "You got whiskers growing out on your lip there." He indicated the corners of his mouth with his fingers. "You're turning into a man already, and right here in the hardware."

"I *am* turning fourteen this year. I'm starting to get whiskers on my chin too, but I shave them off when they come out."

"Welp, it's about time then! Let's check out this shit, and we can get going home before it's dark and the weather gets bad."

On the way home that day, he kept looking over at me and smiling. I kept my eyes focused out the passenger window.

The day after that, he was home from work. I had to pass by his bedroom to get to the bathroom. The door was opened wide and I wondered why it wasn't closed, because he was naked, sitting on the edge of the bed with his white briefs on the floor near his feet. He had a red plaid cloth in his hand covering most of his face and his eyes were closed while he was stroking himself, not even trying to hide it. I couldn't look at that. I walked away thinking he didn't see me, but he called me back.

"Vinny, Vinny, come here! It's all right, son. You can come in. You jack off, right?"

The realization slowly crept up on me that the cloth was my underwear I wore the day before and threw in the hamper. I stared at the floor not saying a word, my heart pounding violently in my chest. I could hear it in my ears. I glanced up for a second. Dad was smiling, sideways, with only one side of his mouth as he did. I wanted to walk away, but that wouldn't do me much good after this point. Dad had already made a habit of talking with me at the end of my bed most nights since Mom died, and he would just follow me to my room.

"So do I! Me and your mom did it even when she was still around. Course she did a lot more than *that*. It's okay."

I still could not talk. I looked up briefly, but then looked back down to the floor tracing the pattern in the floor tiles with my eyes.

"Come on, come on, come in," he said in a whispery, but hoarse voice, smiling that crooked smile. "It's okay."

He remained seated on the bed, but reached his free hand out toward me, his faced fixed, frozen in that smile that was higher on his left side than his right. My feet stepped forward, little steps.

"Come on, come on."

When I was within reach of his hand, he grasped the crotch of my pants, taking my penis and balls gently and pulled me closer to him that way. "I'll show you some things. You can pretend I'm a girl," he said. "You like girls."

I opened my mouth, but at first nothing came out. Then I cleared my throat.

"What is it, son?'

"I know," I croaked.

"You know what, son?" he asked, beginning then to rub my things in an even rhythm.

Again, I had trouble getting the words out. "A-a-about what t-to do."

Dad continued to massage me, and I couldn't help myself.

"I'm sure you do," he said. "They talk about that at school, but have you been with a girl already?"

I shook my head weakly.

"You sure like 'em though. I see you look at them a lot."

Dad stopped rubbing me and stroking himself, and instead hooked one hand inside my pants, and pulled me right up next to him, towing me in between his legs.

"Look at that big banana, I got," he said, looking down at his erection. "That's what mine is shaped like. I think it's pretty. Can you touch it for me?"

We were both silent for a minute.

"Hm?"

I reached my hand forward and brushed it with the back of my fingers.

"Oh, come on! Fucking *touch* it," he said, louder, and so I rubbed it up and down with the back of my fingers. "Yeah, yeah!"

He then started to unbutton my pants, pulling them and my underwear down. My own erection sprung up.

"Yee hah, now there's a late birthday present. Goddam, you got a good-looking cock on you for thirteen and a half."

He made a noise deep in his throat and then dived his head down on my boner, taking it in his mouth and bobbing his head up and down.

I gasped a little, grabbing Dad's shoulders, and then whispered, "Don't."

Dad came off it. "Mmm! See? It's a good thing to have me play a girl, for ya!" The sideways smile returned.

He next took my shirt off, ripping it a bit. I don't know where, even now, but I heard it.

"You're starting to get a few hairs on your chest too!"

I nodded.

"Mmm, I ain't got a lot of that," he said running a hand over his chest, "but I got a hell of a nice body for an old man," he added, nodding.

He then stood up and picked me up, throwing me down on his bed.

"Damn, you smell good, you little bastard."

"I-I'm always clean."

He lay himself on top of me and started kissing my neck and ears. His breath smelled of the gin mom used to drink before bed. His weight on my chest made it hard for me to breathe.

"It's nice having me be a girl for ya, huh?"

I remained silent, but then he got off me to lift my legs up and throw them over his shoulders. He looked down at me.

"You make me so fucking nuts! You know how much I've wanted your ass?"

I did love my dad.

He yanked me up further.

"I want your nuts in my face while I make love to that ass!"

I can't say what I was thinking or feeling about it; my mind was a blank sheet of paper, and I felt hot everywhere. My skin was on fire, like I'd felt when I was sent to the principal's office in school once, and she had to talk to me about my behavior when I knew I was wrong, and the outcome would be bad. I don't think I was able to respond with words.

After he finished with it, he said, wiping his face with my red, plaid boxers, "You can put your clothes back on."

I said, sitting up, "I'm going to take a shower."

Something like that happened a few more times over the week. He bit my shoulder pretty bad one time. In between, I didn't talk to him unless I had to, but he was still being the same old Dad, like before. One of the times he picked me up off the couch and threw me over his shoulder, saying, "You're the girl now" and I was supposed to do to him what I wanted girls to do with me, and sometimes he played the girl, to help me "appreciate tits more" when I could get them in my hands.

By the next weekend, he told me I was going to be the girl "for real and real" and he prepared me for what I was getting, so it would hurt less, but it didn't help much.

"Does that feel good, puppy? Oh, fuck, fuck that makes me so fucking hard."

When he finished doing it all, he was making deep, growling sounds in his throat. "I'm gonna explode inside you, puppy! Oh yeah, fucking bitch boy. Gonna shoot! Gonna Shoot! Fuck. Fuck!"

Afterward, he told me he'd take me to the county fair the next day for being so good about it. He gave me $200 to spend there, but as time went on, and I got older, it happened less often, and by the time I was about sixteen, we both made a kind of covert contract to forget about it, and I tried. I tried to forget many things—not just that—but after I was married and on my own, I'd try to forget everything almost every day, and then the thing came into me and gave over to me its own thoughts, and it had its own special powers of feeling that I wasn't aware of.

As for Dad, after Memorial Day, about two weeks after the thing came into me, he died too. No one could know for certain, but the official report was that he had lost control of his car while driving too fast on the gravel road coming back from the cemetery and went down the hillside into a tree, where the car wasn't visible from the road. They suspected maybe alcohol played a part, but no one could say that for certain either.

The front end of the car was crushed, and the dashboard pinned him to the seat. His legs were broken, and any movement would have been excruciating. Whether it happened that way or not, I was sure that there was pain. I knew pain would be there. No one would likely have been able to hear him call for help, but after about two days, he did finally decide to try for something he could reach—his revolver in the glove compartment.

XII. Anubis

A.

In the two years and seven months before it came into me, this was the situation, as best as I can recall, and as I have read.

The living world, the Earth we live on, could be the real Hades in disguise, Persephone's seasonal queendom, because it's here where things die every day. Not just living beings, but non-living entities, devices, machines, stars, planets, galaxies, particles of dust. They are here, and then they're gone, maybe within a second, sometimes after millions of years, but after some period of time, each thing will be gone. People, animals, and plants, all have an expiration date, but we can't see it. It's hidden under our skin or written in the air hovering over us, and invisible to us, but they can be seen by whatever strange and dark pyxies follow, invisible and silent.

When it's your time, then your time is up. It is no one's fault. Nothing can change it, and nothing can stop it. That's what I believe. Even if you're murdered, it was just your time, someone took it upon themselves, to do the pyxies' bidding. You're dead. That's all there is to know or understand.

Then someone must do something with the body. You can't leave it out in the open, or whatever place it's in, to rot. I'm not sure what happens next. Every time I've been exposed to a death, someone else had taken it from there—Mom, Dad, and so on. I know that someone must make phone calls, and someone comes to take the body away. Those people aren't psychic. I've had to read about what happens next, about what happens to bodies, or what should happen under most normal circumstances, when there is a complete body. I read that the inside of a newly dead body has no smell, but it does, it smells like liver. It does.

If you're going to have a viewing in a funeral home, like Mom had, then the body needs to be embalmed. This doesn't happen when you're cremated, like Dad. The mortician first washes the body in a disinfectant solution and the limbs are massaged and manipulated to relieve rigor mortis, though that lasts no more than a day or two. I'll talk about this more later. The facial hair is shaved, unless the dead person wore facial hair in life. The goal for the funeral director is to create the illusion that the dead body is in happy sleep, even though the mourners know they're not sleeping.

The mortician closes the eyes, sometimes using a glue, and sometimes using flesh-colored oval-shaped eye caps—things that sit on the eye and secure the eyelid in place. The mouth is closed, and the lower jaw is secured by sewing it or with wires. If the jaw is sewn shut, suture string is threaded through the lower jaw below the gums, then up and through the gums of the top front teeth, into the right or left nostril, through the septum, into the other nostril, and back down into the mouth. Then the mortician ties the two ends together.

If the jaw is wired shut, a tool called a needle injector is used to insert a piece of wire anchored to a needle into the upper and lower jaws. The wires are bound together to securely close the mouth. Once the jaw has been secured, the mouth can be molded into something that will pass for natural and peaceful. This is boring, I know, but it's important.

Someone removes the blood from the body through the veins—we need someone to do that for us, to remove blood—please, God—and it's replaced with embalming solution via the arteries. The embalming solution is a combination of chemicals with formaldehyde. The mortician might use dyes in order to simulate a life-like skin tone if there is discoloration. No one would want to look at a purply-grey corpse, though I would. I would've, given the chance. There needs to be a body.

These are facts I have learned. For cavity embalming, a small incision is made near the bellybutton, and a sharp surgical instrument called a trocar is inserted into the body cavity. Using the trocar, organs in the chest cavity and abdomen are punctured and drained of gas and fluid contents and then replaced with the formaldehyde-based chemical mixtures. The mortician closes the incision, and at this point, the body is fully embalmed. This makes it all right, but then a body is buried, when there is a whole body to bury.

The first stage of human decomposition is self-digestion and begins immediately after death. As soon as blood circulation and respiration stop, the body has no way of getting oxygen or removing wastes. Excess carbon dioxide creates an acidic environment, causing membranes in cells to rupture. The membranes release enzymes that begin eating the cells from the inside out. This is okay. It's natural.

Rigor mortis causes muscle stiffening, but it's a temporary condition. Depending on temperature and other conditions, rigor mortis lasts about 72 hours. The phenomenon is caused by the skeletal muscles partially contracting. The muscles are unable to relax, so the joints become fixed in place. Small blisters filled with nutrient-rich fluid begin appearing on internal organs and the skin's surface. The body will appear to have a sheen due to ruptured blisters, and the skin's top layer will begin to loosen.

Next, the body will begin to bloat. Leaked enzymes from the first stage begin to produce gases. The sulfur-containing compounds that the bacteria release also cause skin discoloration. Due to the gases, the human body can double in size. In addition, insect activity can be present. This may take a long time if the body has been embalmed, but it will happen. It is okay. When there is a body, and it was cared for as it should be, then this will not happen until after the body is buried. No one will see it.

The microorganisms and bacteria produce foul odors called putrefaction. This is okay. It's natural. If a body has not been deeply buried, then these odors are what alert others that a person has died, and the smells can linger long after a body has been removed. During putrefaction, the body naturally turns increasingly green, but about eight to ten days after that, the body turns from green to red as the blood decomposes and the organs in the abdomen accumulate gas.

I didn't want to clean what was left behind, but Dad wouldn't do it. No one would, and we couldn't just leave it all down there with the slime.

Back to the normal circumstances. Several weeks after that, the fingernails and toenails fall out. This is okay, this is normal; it is expected. The body starts to liquefy, and most of the body mass is lost over time, until it's a skeleton. There is nothing wrong. It will be okay. No one ever told me it would be okay.

It's a tradition in many cultures that touching a dead body makes you unclean. I washed so much, for a week afterward, but it didn't make any difference. Dad and Bernadette wouldn't even go down there to look afterward. I wouldn't let her do that even if she wanted to. She wouldn't cry in front of me, but instead, she'd suddenly drop what she was doing and run off to sit in the car. I did it—the mopping, the hosing down, and the bleaching.

B.

Too many knives around! Why did Alex have them? I don't know. He had at least one sword that he kept in his room. He claimed it was a claymore, a replica from the Middle Ages. I never saw that one. He said he kept it by his bed. He had too many knives. Not the fancy hunting knives they sell at carnivals or the kind in survival ads, though he had those too, but plain kitchen knives. I saw him cook once, maybe twice, nothing I would ever eat. I ordered food a lot, to pick it up—but he had an expensive knife set in the kitchen by the sink. I was seriously afraid he would stab me one of my nights in the day while I slept. They served no other purpose.

Every time I looked at them—every time—I couldn't help thinking, "How would it feel?" Stabbed repeatedly, being cut cruelly deeply, hurt very badly. Pain was all I could think about then, and without any help. I couldn't get the image of blades and blood out of my mind for long. There was so much blood in a body. What does stainless steel deep in the body feel like? I couldn't keep from feeling it. It was there, flashes—mental images—intruding on my thoughts.

I stayed out of that apartment as much as I could, but sometimes, most often in winter, if the weather was cold, snowy, or wet, there was nowhere else to go or anywhere I wanted to go. I'd curl myself into a ball on the opposite end of the couch. It was set on top of a wooden platform Alex built for it. Yes, when I moved in, the couch was on a crude platform of two-by-fours and plywood, about three feet off the floor that he made himself. He liked to survey the room—what there was of one—and there were no curtains in the windows. I didn't want to stay there long, so I never bought them myself.

Alex never shut up unless he was asleep. When I did want to stay home—and I never thought of that place as home—I couldn't hear what we were watching on TV most of the time. There were only two things he ever watched, and almost every night: True crime shows—someone missing or murdered—and old war movies with predictable plots and clichéd dialogue. Most of those movies were in black and white. The sky wasn't blue. The Mediterranean wasn't green. The countryside was in shades of grey. If I'm going to watch a movie, I want to see the color of things. I put up with two and half, almost three, years of that. He said he had a job at a convenience store. He said he was a student too, but he was home most of the time. I don't know what he did. I didn't care. My mind wasn't on him or what he did with his day.

Bea was his girlfriend, a cute, petite girl with black hair. I don't think that was her real name. Maybe it was just the initial. On most weekends, she'd stay over, and then I'd lose my seat on the couch. We had one wooden chair with a foam cushion on it at the "lower level." Even when I wanted to be in the living room, which wasn't often, they'd purposely make me feel uncomfortable. I don't know how many times they'd be lying next to each other for a while, then she'd look at me and whisper in his ear, so I'd usually go back to my bedroom. It was the size of a walk-in closet—and it probably was one at one time—or maybe a prison cell. I'd read under the stained-glass lamp, and I drank quite a bit while I was there. Being drunk wasn't something that interested me much before, but it did then, and sometimes a lot, because it would make some things easier to take.

Dad would call or come over about once a month and try to convince me to go back to the house. He said I'd be better off, but I wouldn't do that. Besides, Old Harry made me sign the lease at least two months before it ended both years, and since I had nowhere else in mind I could afford, I stayed there.

"Listen—"

My blender drink almost knocked over onto the floor, because I had to bend down so far from his platform to reach it, the glass jar on top tipping sideways until the remainder of the rum-spiked milkshake landed on the coffee table.

"Goddam, dude, watch it! You're cleaning that shit up if it's on the carpet. Old Harry's gonna have a fucking conniption-ass fit if you ruin his carpet. He had 'em installed just the day before you moved in here. I had to move all the fucking furniture out."

"It was hard to get to it from up here."

"And, hey, what's up with that faggy, frozen blueberries bullshit anyway? Have a goddam brewski like a full-grown man with a pair of nuts." Brown dribble from his chew came out of the corner of Alex's mouth. He wiped it off.

I started to get up.

"I mean, not now. Jesus Christ, after you got all that ice cream bullshit in you, you'd be puking like a firehose. Get rid of that shit, dude. Surprised you're not fat as fuck. I mean I'm not in the greatest shape these days. We're gettin' into spring though. I'll be hitting the gym more starting next week, soon's I can renew my membership. What is it? Fuck. The fifth? Hate going out in the fuckin' cold if I don't have to, you know? I know *you* don't. Oh, and if your dad has to visit, man, keep it to when I'm working or in class. No offense, man, you're a cool dude, sometimes, but your dad is creepy as fuck. I don't like the way he looks at me. You know? I mean, I hate to be the one to break it to ya, but I think your dad's some kind of pervert. I mean, I know him and your mom made you and all, but deviants get married and have kids all the time, man. My buddy's mom was married for nine years to his dad, then she left him for a fat-ass dyke with a dick that she went to church with. Not bullshittin' you. She or he was getting surgery to get the meat chopped, but still liked girls. Shit like that happens. But grab a brewski outta the fridge."

"I don't drink beer much. It's too bitter." I stuck out my tongue.

"There's flavored beer, like cherry and apple ale. If you want fancy fruity shit, drink that. It's still beer, man!"

Another night, a few months later:

"You're drinking more than me lately. You sure you're not an alcoholic? I prolly am, cuz I come from a family of 'em." He laughed, then he leaned himself over toward my end of the couch. "So, what happened with your mom? D'you even know? I mean, I know you were young—I donno. Maybe you don't remember, but people talk, you know?" Alex leaned back over to his side. "I'm surprised they never picked him up on that. Not my business, but people talk, ya know. I just don't know why they didn't investigate that shit. I would've if I was in law enforcement." He laughed. "I prolly would'a been a good cop if I didn't smoke so much weed and shit. They prolly don't like that in cops. I'm sure I'd be a good one, but fuck that. I'm not gonna stop being what the fuck I am to pass a drug test. I'd never apply for a job that made me piss test for drugs and shit anyway. You know? You don't even smoke cigs. You didn't even drink before you moved in here. I'm a bad influence on people. Bea tells me that."

He laughed and laughed.

Another night, a few months later:

We were watching one of his crime shows. In the episode a woman—a grown woman—an older woman, on the street was killed by some guy's pair of Cane Corsos. That was followed up by the story of a missing little girl who was never found. That was all I remembered of it and not much of that. They were both true stories, I think. Maybe not, but Alex took all those stories seriously. He was drunk. I think I was too.

"Holy shit! Bet that was fucking bloody. I mean getting mauled like that—guts on the concrete. I know bears are pretty badass that way. They'll shred the fuck out of you. Bite right into your skull. Lions must be bad but bears gotta be the worst."

He froze. A car insurance commercial came on. He pretended to watch it.

After another minute he said, "Man, sorry, dude, I forgot about that with the kid and shit." He went mellow, the one time I'd heard him speak to me with care in his voice. "Fuck, man. That must'a been rough. I can't imagine it. Wanna 'nother beer?"

I didn't want one. I don't know what I wanted. I don't think I ever did.

We were both silent then, and almost every day for a week or so after that, but that night there was nothing else for sure, except eventually, "What did they do with that... your dad's... I mean after it happened?"

Alex tossed his chow mein container over his head, making the basket. "When they're vicious, I'm sure the cops..."

"Dad shot her."

C.

We were on the third floor of a six-unit building, so when I looked out the window of my bedroom, I could look out down onto the yards and gardens of the buildings nearby. It was mid-spring—Beltane, the pagans would say—and all around, every natural thing was both grey and greening at once. The darker the sky became with rain-heavy clouds, the more colorful the damp and landscaped yards and gardens grew.

Those last two months at Alex's, just before it came into me, the world was new, though it was only a few blocks from the apartment I had with Bernadette and the baby. It was freshly formed, like I had never seen that street before, as if it grew up from the ground around me with both weeds and the new-hatched caterpillars to munch them. I was willing to think fond thoughts of her again, because I willed them into my mind, and on that day, the trees had peppered their spindly tops with green buds. Daffodils blasted their yellow trumpets. The clouds as dark as they could be, were happy grey hippopotamuses, dancing to my eyes with the sun peeking out between their giant, round rumps.

I wanted to use pretty words to match the pretty day I woke up to, and they still came to me then, but I had none to give. I wanted magic, and I tried my best, but I was no poet myself, and instead, I found a book of poetry later that same day at the county library, which was almost around the corner, and just that day, by crazy luck, they were selling books on a massive oak table. Maybe that was the magic, yes. Those warmer days made me lazy, but I could still read, and reading was what I did.

I wanted to run outside like a little boy again, and spin in circles in the warm breezes, to play block-wide hide-and-go-seek with the kids from my second-grade class, wherever they were, or maybe go to the zoo or the park and swing on the monkey bars.

The air smelled sharp and sweet. I can't put my finger on the scent, something fresh with junipers berries, but filthy at the same time—metallic, like blood, but God no, not anything cold and unnatural like that. It was more like I imagined salt air by the sea to smell.

The mountain snows had melted into the muddy streams, and alongside them, shoots of flowers and herbs popped up from the ground. Hello to everything, both dreadful and beautiful that I could see. It was only a beginning. Only.

XIII. The Devouring Place

Every place is hell for somebody. Maybe the things we fear, the things that make us mad, the things we love, or say we love, are passed on in our DNA, like the color of our eyes or the shape of our noses. It's possible that somewhere in our brains there's a gene that gets into our blood and passes it on in egg and sperm so that the same fears, out of a sense of human self-preservation get recycled. What our mothers feared, we fear. What we fear, our children fear. My mom was afraid of the same things I was afraid of. Fear always showed, but I feared those things even deeper in my heart.

Everyone in the house was afraid of the dark, damp basement, not just me. Mom refused to keep the washer and dryer down there, so Dad spent a week making a connection upstairs by the back door. He said one time when a breaker flipped that he had to "go down into that god-fucking shitty basement."

Of course, Daisy was afraid of it too, pulling back when she came near the stairs. Dad adopted her from the shelter so he could keep the house safer after I got married and he was there alone. The staff said she needed "TLC" because she was abused as a puppy. She was fiercely protective of him, though, and he took her with him whenever he went out. Later, he'd have to tie her to the base of the stairs whenever anyone came to the house, so they'd be safe from *her*, but there is no safety there for anyone or anything. Poor baby, how could you?

"We'll have to put money into sealing it, eventually" is what Dad said at least a dozen times when I was growing up—and more often after Mom died. "It'll be worth the investment," he said, and then as much as he fixed and remodeled the rest of the house, he never got around to finishing the basement. He thought a game room would be nice down there, to put a foosball table and pool table on one side, a big-screen TV and some comfy furniture, but that never happened. It would never, because our basement wouldn't let that happen, and who would dare play games down there? It wouldn't change for us.

Dad wasn't my father by flesh and bone. He married my Mom before I was six, but you probably already learned that by now. I don't remember. I'm sure I repeat myself a lot, and it's something that happens. I can't believe anymore that Mom knew who my flesh and bone father was, and she refused to talk about it with me. Even when I thought I was old enough to learn the whole story, she would tell me "when you're older." It might just be that there was no story to it at all.

I believe he was a foreigner who could speak Greek, maybe Spanish, and dark, like me. Had he married my mom, the fleshbone dad, the dark, mysterious stranger, from South America or the Middle East, maybe, would have read my books to me at night before bed. He would have been the one to read them to me in a way that I would understand every one, in the way their authors intended their work to be understood, but through his thick accent.

I could have created the pictures in my head without the words getting in the way, instead of me being left alone to drown in their language. Fleshbone Dad would have taken me on those trips on a plane to visit fleshbone Grandma, maybe in India, where we would ride a decorated elephant. He would have been proud of me and dress me up in a miniature three-piece suit with a bowtie to show me off, and he'd have taken me up on his shoulders to watch pretty beauty queens and white-faced clowns in parades.

It leaked down there. It doesn't rain very often, but when it does, it'll come down hard, and the water would seep in through the cracked and porous walls—slimy, thin cascades over calcium sheets, draining into rivers on the floor, like a horror movie alien monster, invading the house in the only way it knew how: inch by inch. There was a drain in the floor, but the little round holes in it wouldn't allow anything past, so the filthy water would just sit over the drain until it evaporated or oozed back to where it came from.

I imagined that one day, if it ever rained hard enough, the entire basement would fill up like a massive pool, but not the glossy, blue water of frolicking nymphs. Instead, it would be a concrete, horror-show tank for filthy fish that swim in filthy water, and unlit, because for certain the electricity would go out. The furnace would then become a giant octopus—that's what it already looked like—and all the slime would float to the top with the squirming, slippery, red, liver-smelling sea creatures underneath. That was something I imagined, and if that happened, someone would doubtless chain me to the top of the stairs like Andromeda preparing to be wolfed down by one of the sickening, boneless creatures as the tide came in.

Dad bought the "white elephant" when I was four or five. I have the haziest memory of moving in. The kitchen was blue then with a border of tiny, yellow dancing flowers. Mom liked the colors and kept them, because they worked with the country theme she was crazy about, so she built on it. The house was in disrepair, Dad said, but freshly painted, inside and out, when it was put on the market. The basement door was grey many years, maybe decades, before we moved in, and no one painted that, so it was cracked and chipped. Mom and Dad didn't touch it, choosing to let it decay in its own time, maybe to go with the country kitchen effect, but even after all the remodeling after Mom died, Dad didn't paint it or replace the door.

If I remember anything about moving into the house, it's in the form of a mental snapshot from behind my own eyelids: I was lying on the hardwood floor in the expanse of the open, empty living room looking up at the ornate ceiling fixture, a Victorian spaceship of bronze acanthus leaves dividing parchment-yellow glass, one of the most beautiful things I had ever seen. I wanted to fly away in it. It looked so far for a small boy—nine hundred feet up, instead of nine.

So, after we moved in, I liked to walk around with a small wall mirror. I would hold it, face up, perpendicular to my body, then look down in it and walk around, so that it felt like I was walking on the ceiling instead of the floor, defying gravity, and making myself sick after a while, but I continued to trek through the entire house feeling that it got me closer to heaven—to the acanthus leaf flying saucer, to the roof, to the sky.

***

The basement was haunted. That's what caused all the fear vibrating in the walls. Black, dagger-toothed demon spirits haunted it—long before me—long before we moved into the house. The demons were there under the ground before the house was built. They spelled it out for us in the house's nature as clearly as if there were words scrawled in red on the basement's concrete walls. The smells of death and burial hit me in the face even at the top of the stairs—mildew, mold, wet dirt, and cobwebs. The air tasted like vinegar in the back of my throat, like a freshly opened jar of pickles, and something dripped somewhere from something that I could never find when I was brave enough to search in midday light.

The smell coming from the floor was like the aquarium my Grandpa and Grandma Thelin had set up the one time I remember being at their house. It was one of my earliest memories, like the acanthus leaf light shade. None of those things are here anymore. Dad broke the glass shade when it went crashing to the floor while he was changing the lightbulb when I was about nine and replaced it with a plain frosted globe. It shattered more thoroughly than glass should ever shatter—thousands of microscopic shards onto the hardwood floor. I wore my shoes in the house for weeks afterward, afraid of cutting myself without realizing it. I asked to keep the metal part. Dad thought it was all right, but Mom thought that there was probably glass inside the channel that held the shade in place, so they both decided we should throw it out. I don't know what happened to Grandma and Grandpa. Like the neighbors, they disappeared after Mom's burial.

And the basement was where Dad had Daisy tied up, in that horrible place where only horrible things could happen. If you don't live in the house anymore, and you come with your wife and toddler to visit, then you don't open that door to see if that dark, damp place has been improved yet, and if you do open it, be mindful to shut it again!

"Vinny! Where's Abby?"

Growling, muffled. Screams, screams, high-pitched alarms, little thing, arching screeching. Daisy, Daisy, what did you do?

"Oh, my God!"

Screams! Horror!

Arms, little toes, pink dress swimming in blood—Daisy lapping that up from the floor—red doll parts! Oh God, poor girl! Bad girl! No!

I learned—I had to learn—that changing houses, moving from one place to another place, doesn't fix a problem! When it's *you* it's been haunting! Wherever you live is exactly where that thing wants to be!

XIV: Lullabye

But a sudden, new life *is* like a miracle. When I held the bottle in the baby's mouth, she would look up to me. She knew who I was.

I helped to make a sweet, little girl with big dark eyes. When she cried from the crib, I ran to her every time, not just to feed her, to change her, or comfort her, but to look at her again, to make sure she was really there.

When she cried, I wanted to hold her in my arms, not just rock her, or rub her belly.

"Don't pick her up every time she makes a noise. She just ate and I changed her. Let her fall back to sleep," Bernadette shouted from the bedroom, groggy, exhausted.

When she first laughed, it was at me. She laughed because I laughed. So, I laughed again, and she laughed again.

It's so easy to make her happy. Bernadette was worn out, but I was a happy daddy.

"Treat her like a little grown-up," Dad said. "That'll raise her right for a tough world."

She did peek-a-boos, and the shy, flirty looks that babies make. I kissed the top of her head so many times, and I took her for walks in the stroller in the park, while the same old women sitting on the bench each day watched and shook their heads. I took time out of a day, each day, for that. Was I doing it right?

"Bernadette, come watch Abby. Vinny's wandering off with her. No, you should bring her over here," I would hear Gabriella say.

I danced her in the air, turning her back and forth. She laughed more and more, with the silly smile with two tiny teeth coming up from the bottom. I took a sick day once to try taking on day-long diaper duty. What could I do wrong?

And I see now, and I know now, that I forgot nothing. There *was* no forgetting. I'd only hoped, with all my heart, to lose my memories. I wished for it, and so I will.

XV. Dagger of The Mind

Whatever the circumstances, it spoke and continued to speak, whispering in my ear, but it was difficult at times to tell, and certainly not then, not until lately or too late. When it spoke, maybe it wasn't into my ear, but from somewhere inside of it, from the clanging of the hammer to anvil—the smithy tools of the head—and out through the drum, *boom boom boom*—in reverse order, nonsense and gibberish, maybe, but also in many languages of the world, the languages of devotion. It knows them all, and to respond to them all in amused chatter with itself like a child playing alone with its toys. Whether it understands, or I understand never mattered; it assumes I do, and I always did.

The thing said many times—in words I understood—that it meant harm only to those I said I love, that I believed I loved, or that I felt shame over loving, whichever case they fell into, but it claims to mean no harm to me, never in any way, and for the most part the thing had been quiet today, but there are certain things I honestly had forgotten. My mind was in a bell jar of vapors, and I sometimes imagined more than I recalled. The image behind my eyelids would see the thing as a pretty girl, fully grown and developed, with pale blonde hair and a lilting laugh, something I could ease myself into. She's there curled up in my heart. That is what I liked to think.

I mean to you no harm.

But it lied. It was a bribery. Not only is she a bitch, but a briber, or blackmailer. I'm not so sure of which, because it was offering nothing and had no dirt on me, but please don't throw dirt on me yet. I have been good. I have been as good as I could be for all of twenty-six years. That's almost ancient, and I am still trying to do the best I can.

You are a good boy.

So maybe it's neither, or maybe both.

Its voice is hoarse and shrill. Both of those at the once, like a death yelp of—I don't know—if that can be imagined, with heavy breath punctuating its words, as if each one were its last.

Finally, I remembered what the word was that I was looking for. It hadn't yet taken that thought away from me: Mortgage—or *mortgagee*. That's what the curse was—the thing was an extortionist, demanding blood for relief. A black and menacing mortgagee, it whispered over and over and over what I must do to stop their pain—Bernadette's and Gabriella's pain—and anyone else who might follow, anyone that I might love again—and here I am with the opportunity. It was too late for Dad, and what could I have done? Dad was a warning to prove the rule. He was expendable to the thing. It was a way to prove to me that this was not all in my mind. Not a game to play. It wasn't something to be toyed with.

Come on, boy! Come on, boy!

A deep, deep guttural growl and a shriek, again, inside my head. It explodes and then bubbles over like a volcano. It was so clear and simple; it meant no harm if I was a good boy and I did as I was told, and I had never harmed anyone until then. I swear I didn't, not on purpose. The basement door was an accident that day. The kind I never made again. I didn't mean it.

So now, the two of us, my little girl and I, crossed the kitchen to that open doorway together. Much of the grey paint had skinned off the door by then, showing patches of green underneath. I stood at the top of the wooden stairs, then I looked down at the top of her head. I needed to be strong. She needed to be strong.

"You know, Abby, that I used to be afraid of the basement more than anything?"

She was silent for a moment, before she looked up at me with a frown. Her voice was loud but quavering. "Can I be the daddy now?"

"You could be a mommy, I think, but why *would* you be? Why would *anyone* be?"

"I don't want to be Abby," she said, glancing down the stairs.

"But I need you to be! I'm a big boy and you're a big girl!"

"I want to go with my *real* daddy *now*!"

"I *am* real! I *am*!"

She began to pull back, and I will have to admit, anger was boiling up in me. I couldn't be that. It would have ruined it all for everyone.

"You are Abby now. And forever! Please!"

My girl stared at me. "No," she said and shook her head. I couldn't read her expression. Her mouth had dropped open, at first not in fear, but shock. I could see her little lower teeth.

What is the thing telling me? Am I the thing? Is *it* the thing?

"Please!" I said, holding her by the wrists.

She began to scream—a high-pitched, eardrum-piercing squeal.

"No, I *cannot* do it now!" I shouted to it, wherever it was.

Necesito que esto esté terminado! You'll ruin it for everyone!

The thing was back, screaming at *me* now because in my heart, I was a coward. Bad words for bad people end in A-R-D.

It laughed. I'm sure I never heard the thing laugh before.

Bastard!

Drunkard!

Buzzard! That old buzzard! It flies in circles over me!

Coward!

Yes, coward!

I could no longer tell the difference between Abby's screams at the end of my hand and the screams of the thing from within my own ear, but it all had to end tonight.

And even now she stared, eyes wide open, mouth gaping, inching backward away from the basement doorway.

Do you love her? Tu la ami?

"COME ON, PLEASE!" I tried to compose myself. I lowered my voice. I lied. "Nothing bad is going to happen."

¿La amas?

She then pulled her hand from mine and darted like a terrified, feral cat across the kitchen, and she was so lithe and thin, I swear she would have made it up the curtains to the top of the window frame. I had no choice but to chase the little cat as she reached the doorknob, but I had locked the door, and the chain was on.

I dashed across the room, not so much running as floating or flying. My feet, if they were there, didn't touch the floor. At first, I had gotten my fingers tangled in her thin, silky hair, and this only made her scream louder, but I then I managed to grip her wrists again, like a vise.

I thought I was a weak, sniveling thing, but my brain tricked my arms into believing that they were stronger than they were. I focused as much as I could on my personal mission of freedom that I could now make right by an unnecessary wrong. So, taking her—both arms—we flung her into the empty space at the center of the doorway. In the act, I stubbed my baby toe against the door frame, but the basement door was open! It was open! If I had locked it, it would not have worked. There was seamlessness in the substitution. There was no doubt.

The light from the kitchen spilled out no further than the top of the stairs, so I could see nothing. She must have first hit the wall overhanging the stairs, because we heard a hollow knock first, though we didn't have the courage to look. Then she must have hit the slimy cement floor because we heard no more than a dull thump or thud, like a watermelon. After that sickening smack, I heard nothing else, no cries, no baby's horrified squeals, no strangulated screams, no teeth, just silence.

The thing should be satisfied, I'm sure. This corrected everything. The pain should end. I gave it what it demanded. I'm doubly sure. It wanted intention. I listened. I behaved. I followed what it told me to the letter. It would be over.

XVI. Carmen et Error

I'll bet it's not raining where you are, if you're anywhere. It started raining here some time ago. I wish I could say when it was, but it began coming down hard. I could hear it beating on the windows and on the roof. Its steady, muffled sound is like static on a car radio. I went to the window to see if there was any flooding, but the water washing down in sheets on the pane made it impossible to see the yard or street.

Oh my God, I could be wrong, but I think there was a knock on the door just before the rain started up, but the red and blue lights were gone, at least for now, and aside from the rain, it has been quiet. I wish there were peace with the rain. There was for me a few times but never here. I have the familiar books, if just for the pictures, which are almost as calming as a family photo album, and it takes my mind off of it.

After I found a hardcover copy of *Ulysses* last year at a yard sale, I tried to read it cover to cover. I know you don't care about that. You never cared about the book thing, but I wasn't a success with reading it. I was at Alex's place then and decided to read a chapter a week to escape, even though he tried each night to get me to come out of my room "to hang out." I did finish it, but it was too difficult to read much in one sitting. I had a hard time sticking with it. It's a complicated book to read for anyone of any age.

What is a Martello tower? Right from the beginning, I had to stop to look it up. It doesn't seem like something people would live in. I don't know anything about Dublin in the 1920s, so I had to read about that too, about how the British treated the Irish then. It was all relevant to the story and that tied it together. Because the writing was complex, it was intriguing, even at places where I didn't understand it. I liked the way Joyce wrote it, with a surprise on every page, especially the one long sentence at the end. Reading a little every day made the difference.

Did you know that in Norway, there is a castle called Akershus? It's somewhere outside of Oslo. I saw it on TV. I watch it once in a while now, since reading's become almost impossible. I relearned how to turn the TV on and off, but that's about all. The castle was built to house and protect the royal family, but today it's a museum. I thought you might be interested in this, because one corridor is haunted by a large, mad black hound, named Malcanisen who was buried alive long ago in the Maiden's Tower on the east side, near the old main entrance of the castle, so that the animal could stand guard. I imagined many times what that must be like. You'd like Norway. I can see it as being wild, and cold, and wooded—all the things you enjoy. What else?

I found that poetry book—*Real Poems for A Real World: An Anthology*—that I was reading earlier this year, but not so much reading as using, I guess. I memorized the title, so I know that much. I'd purposely buried it under a pile of newspapers at one point, because it shouldn't have been there. It should have been with the other books, but no, it was buried. I suppose I buried it, but I can't remember. I can't remember when I'd last seen the book either, but I knew where it was. It was easy to uncover; I just can't say why I needed to find it.

I opened the book to one page that it almost fell open to on its own, and I looked at the words. Words and letters are pretty on their own without even being able to read them. They form delicate, dancing shapes. I did read the poems in it before my senses fell off like they did, and I liked them—some of them—though I'm not usually interested in poetry. They were all written by students and teachers in the area. Anyway, words are pretty, creating swaying patterns on the page, like flowers on wallpaper. What I never found was the Easter egg picture.

Here's the first page I opened to. I understood it before all of this, but now it's a jumble of words with *human, human, human*.

Sisters of Charity Hospital
by Harold Oldeman
I watched a doe today. She walked the streets
as a whore in spotted brown.
She was wounded in human, about human,
from human form
She glanced through the unseeing taxi traffic,
as if to say "genau."
"In perpetuity. In domination.
Your name anew is Christ."

> *So, the sensei said, then sighed and repeated, "Let me walk with him"*

Eternity is a glimpse of animal husbandry.
Let me walk with him.
Something like companions.
Let me walk with him.
Something in between.
Divided by the yod of indifference.
It is enthusiastic. Like a parent country
or the Y of control.
It is atomic. Or a pusher.
Lowering. Expansive. Absolute.

Active. Unwound. Disruptive. Destroyed.
I watched a doe die in the street.
She said "genau," I think.
In the hum of chaos. I think I fell in love.

All right, and then there is this one, longer and narrower. It's graceful with words.

The Watercolor Class
by Wendy Marie Gorniak
By the end of summer,
the hunter can no longer
sense the depth and chill of winter.
Each tree,
oak, maple, and ash
with shimmering tresses
bright green
and shining
where once, bare-armed,
they shook from cold.
Beneath one March maple
The former dancer stood
with concave cheeks
unlike before
Scars on his wrists
and unlike before
The plaid flannel fell freely
As leaves from his skin.
Both victims of the wind
He reminded me
that winter would soon succumb
To spring

*And so, I pictured myself
reclining on a slab beneath
A wind-blown yew
Watching the surf crash,
Against the stony cliffs below
But it was only a bonsai.*

And this on the page across from it with a spot of cranberry juice from my thumb, near the top of the page.

Interchange
by Eric Bee
*My course altered
and you traveled without me.
The interchange was seamless;
imperceptible to most.
But I, I was not so ignorant;
not so…blissfully unaware.
Your footsteps echoed within me-
a shadow of vicious indifference.
And you, you danced unimpeded;
gracefully…in dauntless revelry.
Into my fading horizon, you vanished-
just another memory to forget.*

Ghost of A Dog
by Vincent Something Pelletier
I HAD NO CHOICE IN THIS MATTER,
MA'AM, SIR
YOU TOLD ME WHAT I MUST DO!
NOW AM I ALONE? NEVER NEVER
MY ONLY, LONELY LOVE
WITH SOLITUDE COMES FREEDOM

NO
PLEASE DO NOT EVER LEAVE ME
PLEASE DO NOT EVER LEAVE ME
PLEASE DO NOT EVER LEAVE ME
I DO NOT KNOW WHICH I WANT MORE!
YOU ARE ALL I HAVE

I know what innocence looks like. It is exactly like that. I don't know what to think anymore. Everything is like my other true love; I want to be rid of it, but it is all I have. I don't want it to leave me alone, not with all this. I'm not sure where I am. Maybe I'm still at the house. I must be, because I know where my things are when I need to find them, but there are now lights where there shouldn't be lights and continuous, but hushed sounds, like something trying to dig its way out of the earth beneath me. It's never quiet. There are always strange voices echoing outside, and I wonder if I am, in fact, not home, although I feel so. I'm watching my life after it was filmed through a Vaseline-covered lens, and I am tied to the chair, to watch it again and again and again, until I vomit.

No! The thing won't leave! It told me, in a calm, even tone, like I had never heard come from its maws before, "No, my sweet poochie boy, you did it so wrong. You cheated. You little cheater."

Tu es un petit tricheur.

I hung all our pictures up again, but I put away the one with Daisy, so I could talk to you and the others in private. Without those, it would be lonesome and dreary in the white elephant. I was lucky enough to find one of Gabriella and Bruce, the one you took after we got married, and another of Bernadette in bed in the maternity ward. I put those on the wall too. God, no, wait. It's not right. I'm missing something, something that hasn't happened.

I'm so sorry, Dad. I'm sorry, ladies. I am sorry to everyone for what I did, but there was no other way for me to make it all right. That was what I thought, but escape... it's not so easy. You know those paranormal investigators that you hear about or see on TV? They say spirits haunt a specific place and never leave. They wander the room where they died, and then they're bound to that place for eternity believing they're alive until somehow supernaturally evicted, but I learned that's wrong.

El asesinato debería haber sido más sangriento.

Those investigators are right that spirits never leave, but they can haunt people as well as places. They can follow us, live inside of us, and around us. They lurk in the closets and under the bed, as any small child knows. They can be wherever we can be. We hear the things scratching on the walls. We say it's the house settling, responding to wind and temperature. That's not true either. The thing, my thing, is howling inside the house somewhere when it is not in me, and at times, it is not, but then I wish it were.

Qui la trouvera et emportera son corps ce soir ?

When it roams the house, it *enjoys* the musty dark basement. It has great strength; it's never, ever afraid, like we are. Sometimes it lies awake in dim and untidy rooms, the corners of unused spaces where the sunlight can't reach, and then I lie on the floor searching to meet its glowing eyes that startled me in the beginning. It creeps, crouched down, up the stairs at night, drooling and moaning, and I hope one day the *real* people, the people that I see from day to day, can forgive us, not only me, but me and Daisy. There was nothing else I could do. I had no choice, because the thing followed me home, and then it made me see that I did not kill one that I loved, but one I barely knew. Before I go, I want you to know why I did what I did. Just call me Daisy now because we are one and the same. We are the same animal.

~

~

<u>Acknowledgments</u>
Editor:
Theodore Webb
Those who offered creative guidance:
Stephanie Collins
Kitty Candelaria
Eric Bee
Travisd Simmons
Scott Emerson
Amber Benincosa
Josh Brooks
Devil Doll
Kristi Kelley
J. Chris Lawrence
Catherine Goffreda Bailey
Dr. Andrew Nelson
Anton Abela
Jeffrey L. Buford Jr.
Teachers and those who assisted with research:
Dr. Donna Long
Lorri Gifford
Travis Yow
Dr. Susan Kelley

~

~

Inspiration:
Ulysses by James Joyce
The Chautauqua County Fair
Fr. Rafael V. Baylón, S.J.
"Dreamsleep" by Attrition
BJ's Downwind Café, Fredonia NY
The works of Claude Debussy
The films of David Lynch
Travis Yow
The Other by Thomas Tryon
Dawn McArthur
"The Owl Service" by Pram
Cover art:
Anton Abela
Poetry contributor:
"Interchange" by Eric Bee
Other poems by the author

~

~

About the Author

Steven Anthony George was born in Dunkirk NY and currently resides in Fairmont, WV. He has been previously published in several online and print journals in short fiction and poetry. His short stories were anthologized in *Diner Stories: Off The Menu* (2015) and *Twice Upon A Time: Fairytale, Folklore, & Myth. Reimagined & Remastered* (2015). He is an autistic adult and active in the autism community, often speaking and writing on the topic.

Read more at www.stevenanthonygeorge.com.

Lightning Source UK Ltd.
Milton Keynes UK
UKHW011058060223
416537UK00009B/2280